One Moonlit Night

Pearl Lake, the Moonlit Trilogy

book one

Tina Marie

This is a work of fiction. Names, characters, businesses, places, events, and incidents are either the products of the author's imagination or used in a fictitious manner. Any other resemblance to actual persons, living or dead, or actual events is entirely coincidental.

DEDICATION

To a dream fulfilled.

PROLOGUE

It had been so long since Nancy Quinn had seen her son, Ben. Here he stood in her kitchen, after a long six months of him being in the States.

She drank in his features like a parched man in the desert. She noted the tiredness about his green eyes... eyes she fell in love with the second she held him in her arms. They reminded her of the tender, new growth of springtime ferns. She was his mother, his confidant, his protector from the world. When he was hurting, she was hurting and right at this moment, she knew something was wrong. She was determined to find out exactly what it was that put that scowl on his once carefree, boyish features. *Manly features*, she silently corrected herself. Admitting he was a man now was sometimes hard to do. Doing so meant that she herself was aging, something that Nancy Quinn didn't do.

"Ben, sit, sit yourself down. Are you hungry? I'll make us some tea. How does that sound?"

"Sounds wonderful mum, but first, I need a hug."

She eagerly met him halfway, embracing him for the boy that he was. She loved the fact their hugs always made the world right, even for just for a moment. As she stroked his brown hair, so much like his father's, she held on a little longer, a little tighter, breathing in his scent, memorizing it all for the times he wasn't there. Breaking free, Nancy took a step back, holding his face in the palm of her hands, staring intently into his eyes. She noted the dark circles and couldn't help but ask, "What's wrong? You seem a bit tired."

Oh, how she wished he'd take a break. Ever since his last relationship ended years ago, he had thrown himself into his work. Filming movie after movie, he had distanced himself more and more.

Nancy feared he had become bitter towards women. She couldn't blame him though, not after what that girl had done to him.

Ben reached up and placed his hands on her wrists. With a gentle reassuring squeeze, he responded, "I am, Mum. I'm just tired." He turned to sit at the table.

That wasn't it, there was more. It worried her that the strain of acting was taking a toll on her only child. She had to find out. With a concerned tone in her voice she spoke. "Ben, Hun, I know when something is bothering you, and it's more than just you being tired. Out with it now. Stop skirting around."

Oh, no… when she used that tone, he knew there was no escaping her queries. He desperately sought something to say, to placate her enough that he didn't need to go into any details. To be honest, he was tired. Tired of all the attention. He thought he was ready for Hollywood. And he was, but what came with being famous was not something he thought anyone could ever be ready for. He felt like a fraud. He loved acting, getting into character. What he didn't love was the attention. He was from a small rural town where everyone knew everyone, including their business. They were a close-knit community that felt like family and didn't care who he was, nor were they afraid to say it. But being famous, people threw themselves at your feet. Each one clamoring for your attention. It was just getting to be too much, and he needed a break from it.

"Nothing, Mum," he finally answered, "Not really… you know… just life." *There, that should do it.* It was vague enough not to give anything away, but not lying to her either.

That wasn't the answer she was expecting, nor one that she was settling for. Knowing he'd open up over a nice cup of tea, she grabbed the kettle, filling it with water before setting it on the stove, with a hurried clatter.

"Hmm, right!" she responded, placing the cream and sugar on the table, followed by the cups and saucers. He was just sitting there, his head bent down with his nose in his cell. Tea would not cut it; she was afraid. A memory from days gone by flashed in her mind. *...Cake!! That will surely get him talking...* or, at least it always did when he was a teen. She swiftly went into the pantry to retrieve the cake. *He's a goner now*, she thought, unsuccessfully trying to smother a giggle.

Ben sat with his phone in his hand. He wasn't doing anything on it, just sitting there with it in his hand, staring at it. He hoped his mother would think he was too busy and wouldn't keep hedging for answers. He knew what she was up to. Without moving his head, he looked up to watch her. She was acting a bit strange, to say the least, flighty you might say, muttering to herself as she went about to fix the tea.

Quickly, she turned to the table and just as quickly, he glanced back down at his phone. He snuck a look when she had her back to him. With a cocked brow, he watched in disbelief as she glided to the pantry and... *was that a... giggle? She's up to something.* With the horrifying realization, it hit him at once. *Good Lord, she's getting the damn cake!*

"Darling, look what I have for you."

With dread, he looked up from his phone, leaning back in his chair as she placed a slice before him. "Mum. You didn't have to go to all this trouble."

"No trouble at all," she replied grinning. "So, tell me, how is the shooting going on that new film you're in?"

Oh God, this was the moment he dreaded most. He immediately started digging into the cake, stalling for time.

"I know you love my cake so, but aren't you going to take a breather and answer my question?" she frowned in dismay.

3

He risked a glance at her. There she was, standing with hands on her hips, head tilted to the side, one foot tapping impatiently, waiting for his response. She reminded him of a mother hen. The once knowing smile was replaced with a frown that wrinkled her brow, her eyes staring intently at him as if he were a bug. With a quick cough, he stifled the chuckle that escaped past his lips.

It wasn't that he didn't want to answer her, but he knew once she found out that he had a month off from filming she would insist he stay home. He had other plans frankly, on the other side of the world, to be exact. Finally, he decided there was no escaping the truth. It was time to tell her. Taking a deep breath as he was about to respond, the kitchen door opened with a loud bang. In walked Greg Quinn, his dad, with his arms full of bags. Ben got up to give him a hand. His tension melted away, instantly replaced with relief. His backup had just arrived.

"Benny boy! My God, you're a sight for sore eyes." His dad set the bags on the floor to hug him. Stepping back, holding on to his dad's arms, Ben leaned back to look at him.

"You as well, Dad. You have no idea." He grinned at him.

He took a quick glance at his mom to see her reaction. Yup, the frown was still there. At that moment, his mom spoke up.

"Here now, let's get these things put away so we can have tea," she stated impatiently.

Sitting in the cozy kitchen with his parents with the sun streaming in, Ben realized how much he missed them.

"So, Ben was just about to tell me how that new film he's in is going, weren't you Ben?" his mother said, tossing a pointed look his way as she sat down. She was getting impatient again.

"Um, yeah. Actually, … It's going well. I have some free time coming my way." *There… it was out, mostly.*

He could see the excitement on his mother's face. "Oh? How long? What are your plans? You can stay here!!" Her words tumbled out faster than he could respond.

"Nancy, for heaven's sake, calm yourself down and let the

boy answer you!" Greg cut in.

"Right, yes! Of course," she nodded her head. "I'm just so happy," she added, clutching her hands to her chest. She was fairly dancing in her seat.

Ben looked from one to the other. He hated to disappoint his Mum. Her excitement over the thought of him being home was almost his undoing. For a fleeting a second, he thought about canceling his trip. He looked at his dad, noted the slight shake of his head, and saw the understanding behind his wise eyes. At that moment, Ben knew he'd support his decision.

Clearing his throat, he took a deep breath and said, "I have a month off, possibly longer. It depends on how fast they get done filming the next scenes. Most of mine are finished. I just have to go back for a week or so."

Greg sensed his wife was about to go off again, he held out a staying hand to let Ben finish.

"As for my plans… I um…" He frowned, knowing this would be the most difficult on his mum. "I have booked a trip to Canada… Ontario to be exact." Fearing his mother would interject at any moment, he hurriedly went on.

"You know Mark Donovan?" he glanced up, meeting their gazes. "Well, he had a house on the shores of Pearl Lake that he was planning to sell, a nice piece of property. It backs onto the lake with a bit of land." He paused for a moment. "And I purchased it from him. I plan to stay there… alone. To get things sorted out in my mind, you know?" He hated how even to his ears; desperation was in his voice.

His mum's chair shot out, and in one fluid motion, she was standing. Before anyone could react, she burst forth. "You bought a house without even seeing it first?" she cried out in disbelief.

"Nancy, for God's sake! Sit down and quit being so dramatic," Greg replied in his calm demeanor.

Before his mum could add anything to her line of questioning, he took out his cell phone and brought up pictures to show them. "Here, have a look and see for yourself." It was the first thing he had ever purchased of any significance and he was proud.

There stood a quaint gray sided home with an impressive white stone chimney gracing the outside wall. Sunlight dappled through the massive shade trees scattered around the yard. One could view the lake beyond from the wraparound porch.

His dad was the first to break the silence. "It looks like a beautiful spot, son. I especially love that porch, and I bet the fishing is superb."

His mum took the phone, with tears in her eyes. She silently looked through the photos. It was a lovely spot indeed, but Canada? It was so far away from England.

"Why are you going by yourself? Can't you take someone with you? We could go with him, right, Greg?" She looked to him, hoping he'd agree. Instead, she was met with a shake of his head.

"No, we can't. This is something Ben needs to do on his own. Once he gets things sorted out, then and only then will we make the trip." He looked to Ben for encouragement. "Sound good, son?"

"Absolutely." Ben smiled at him, relieved. "Let me get settled, take a breather for a bit." He pursed his lips, "Downtime, you know what I mean, mum?" He held his breath in anticipation of his mother's response.

Nancy came to understand that there was more bothering her son than a purchase on a whim. He was under so much pressure from everyone; he didn't need it from his mother too.

With a sad nod of her head, she said, "I do. I am sorry for my outburst. Please forgive me." She pasted a smile on her lips. "But enlighten me, if you will. Is this going to be a year-round home?"

He could see the concern etched on her face. Carefully he chose his words to save her from further worry. "I'm not sure, to be honest. The way I travel from location to location... no place is year-round." He could see that she weighed his response.

"Hmm, that is true. One other thing… whatever are you going to do about the bears?"

The answer to that was a quick bark of laughter from both her men.

"*What*? There are bears in Canada; it's an honest question." Well, at least that boyish grin was back on his face.

With a relieved sigh, Ben grinned. "Mum, let's have our tea, shall we, and I'll tell you all about it."

Nancy wiped the tears from her eyes. Giving him a watery smile, she nodded. *Maybe he will finally meet someone who loves him for himself and not the actor.*

CHAPTER 1

Ben arrived in Canada much later than planned. He opened the door to the house, kicking it closed. He dumped his suitcases inside and made his way to the first bedroom he came to. Stripping the dust cloth back, he collapsed into a heap of exhaustion. Never again would he make such a long and arduous journey.

Despite the exhausting trip, it took him forever to fall asleep. The silence was deafening. The darkness was so black that he had a hard time seeing his hand in front of his face. Finally, a fitful sleep overtook him.

The sun slowly crept over the trees, shining on the mirror-like image of the lake. Ben searched the cupboards for some tea but instead found some instant coffee. Unscrewing the lid, he peered into the jar, finding it to be passable. Making a cup, he took the steaming mug out to the porch to soak it all in. He'd been sitting there quietly contemplating what to do for the day, when a doe came cautiously out of the woods. He held his breath in anticipation of her next move, when a fawn came stumbling out, on its mother's heels. Knowing at that moment there was no place he would rather be, he sat there silently, watching them until they took their leave.

He headed into the house to unpack. His stomach rumbled with pangs of hunger. He realized it had been a full day since he had eaten anything. He grabbed his cell and sent a quick text to Mark, asking him if there were any restaurants or stores within walking distance.

Setting the cell down, he busied himself stripping the dust cloths off the furniture. He looked around in disgust. Man, there's dust on everything. He should have taken Mark's advice and hired a cleaning crew to come in. At the time, he didn't think it would be necessary, planning on doing it all himself. But as he looked around, he regretted that decision immediately. With a sigh, he began sweeping the floor and started choking on the dust within minutes. He threw open all the doors and windows to clear the cloud. He turned and headed back to the laundry room to grab the shop vac he saw earlier. *Right! This will work much better.*

Four hours later, he was finishing up mopping the floor when his stomach was rumbling again. He knew there was nothing in the refrigerator but looked anyway. Patting his pockets in search of his cell phone, he remembered he left it on the back of the couch. Four missed calls from his mum and one from Mark. He punched in Mark's number, thinking he would call his mum in a minute. Right now, food was his main priority.

Walking to the store called Mackwells, Ben dialed his mum up. It would be 10 pm in England, but he knew she'd likely be nuts by now with worry, waiting for his call. On the third ring, she picked up.

"Oh, my goodness Benjamin Quinn, are you trying to drive your mother crazy with worry? I was just about to book a flight to Canada!"

"Hello to you too, Mum," he smiled…*And what would you have done when you arrived?* "How's it going?" he replied with a chuckle.

"Don't you dare laugh at me, young man, it's been days since you left home."

Sobering up, he apologized and explained the reasons he was so late in calling her.

Rounding the corner to the store he said, "Look, mum, it's getting late there. Get some sleep, please. I'll call you in a few days, okay? ... I love you too, goodnight." He hung up just as he pushed the door open, hearing a bell signal his entrance. A burly, older man was standing behind the counter while two teenaged girls sat at it drinking milkshakes. *Oh crap, this is the moment.* He steeled himself for the screams of recognition as all three glanced his way.

"Hey there, stranger," the man said. "Are you just passing through or visiting for a spell?"

"Um... Hi there! I'm settling in, actually," he replied, chancing a glance around.

"Settling in you say? Where might that be? By the way, the name's Mackenzie Wells, but everybody calls me Mack," he said, offering his hand.

Reaching out, Ben grasped Mack's in a firm handshake.

"Ben... Ben Quinn. I just bought the place on the point at the water's edge." He tilted his head in the general direction of his home.

"You don't say? Hmm... that place has been empty pretty close to three years now. Didn't know it went up on the market."

"Ah, it didn't. A friend of mine was planning on selling it and I grabbed it up the minute he told me about it," he said with a pleased grin.

"Well, happy to have you here. You want a bite to eat? ... On the house, as a welcome to the neighborhood kind of thing. We have the best burgers and fries around these parts.... won't take but a few minutes to whip it up for you," Mack offered.

His offer floored Ben. He could tell that Mack didn't know what he did for a living, nor did the teenage girls sitting at the counter. It was nice to be treated like a nobody for once.

"A burger and fries sound just about perfect, thanks!" he accepted graciously. "Do you mind if I pick up a few things while it cooks?" he raised his brows, jerking a thumb towards the grocery area.

"Sure, you go right ahead. I'll yell for you when it's just about done," Mack spoke over his shoulder as he headed to the kitchen.

Ben grabbed a shopping basket sitting near the door and headed towards the grocery area, filling it as he went. Deciding to grab the rest after he had eaten, he sat down at the counter to wait for his food. He was studying the dessert menu when he heard a shy, soft, "Excuse me."

Glancing up, he turned to the teenagers and said, "Yes?"

"Um, ah… we just wanted to tell you we think you have a nice voice, like your accent," they giggled in unison.

"Why thank you," Ben replied with a smile, sending the girls into a giggling fit again.

"And you're cute, too," they tossed in for good measure.

"Girls leave the man alone, in peace. Get going home now. I know you both have chores to do," Mack stated, as he placed a heaping plate of food before Ben.

"Sorry about that," Mack said, as the girls took their leave.

"It's fine, really, at least they were polite about it." Ben chuckled as he dug into his food. With every bite, he savored it. He was either extraordinarily hungry, or this was the best food he had ever eaten. He was thinking it was both.

Munching on a fry, he called out, "Hey Mac, can you tell me a bit about the area?"

Mack came from the kitchen, wiping his hands on a towel.

"Well, this side of the lake is mostly a vacation retreat for the rich. There are a few cabins up the road; more like mini mansions if you ask me. They come late spring every year and stay until Labour day then head back. Some come and go throughout the season and some stay year-round, but not too many. In a couple of weeks, you'll see more traffic. The lake will be a busy place, too. Across the water and up a bit there are rental cabins and a camping site. You'll hear it soon enough." Mack continued. "Keep an eye out though. They like to come to this side of the lake and cause a little havoc from time to time."

"What sort of havoc?" Ben questioned. *Great, that's all I need.* He could already feel the tension at the thought.

"Nothing too serious. Mostly just trespassing, cutting through the private properties along the waterfront. Although Abbi Peterson, your neighbor, had a break-in a few months back. She came home after a week away to her door kicked in. Her dog was nowhere around. She found her a day or so later over at your place, huddled on the porch. They never found out who did it," Mack said, shaking his head.

Almost choking on his food, Ben's brows shot up with a quick flash of anger. "Wait... *what*? She left her dog alone for a week?" he asked incredulously. He had a soft spot for dogs.

"Oh, well, she had a house sitter staying to take care of Lucy while she was away. Just so happened that she had stepped out for a bit, knowing Abbi was coming home that day. Abbi has since alarmed the place and has cameras inside and out to catch every angle. I can't say I blame her one bit, with her job. It can bring out the wackos, if you know what I mean?"

Confused, Ben nodded his head in agreement. The way Mack made it sound, it was like he should know who this Abbi was. He hadn't a clue and wondered if he should ask. Mack must have surmised from the look on his face he didn't, because he pointed to the wall.

"Right over there is where you'll find her work," he stated.

Ben turned around to where Mack was pointing. "Oh, so she's a writer, is she?"

Standing up from the stool, he set off towards the book section. He could use a good read to pass the time. Not like he'd bother with her book, though. *She's likely some boring historical romance novelist that writes about the 1300s British royalty... the kind of book my mother would love to read,* he thought with derision.

"She sure is... our Abbi. And a damn fine one, too. That one right there is being made into a movie as we speak." Mack proudly beamed.

"You don't say?" Ben murmured, a bit surprised, as he searched out the titles looking for something that caught his eye. He picked up a book that looked interesting by the front cover, not bothering to read the title. He flipped it over in his hands to see the back. A black-and-white photo of an attractive woman stared back at him. Very attractive, he noted. He checked the inside back cover to find the 'about the author' section and skimmed through it...

Abbi Stevens started her writing path later in life. Having started her family at the tender age of 16 with twin boys and soon to follow a girl. She felt raising her family was more important than her dream. Never giving up hope, she accomplished that dream at age 41. Abbi hails from Windsor, Ontario, Canada, where she lives with her husband and loyal companion, Lucy.

Hmm, no way does she look her age, he thought.

Closing it, he started to read the back cover. A feeling of familiarity came over him as he read. *Wait.... What?* He flipped it over to read the title. 'The Jasper Killings' by Abbi Stevens.

"Uh, hey Mack! What did you say Abbi's last name is?" Ben asked, confused.

"Peterson. But she goes under the pen name of Abbi Stevens," was the answer.

He glanced around in dawning disbelief. "Bloody hell!" he snickered.

"Something wrong, Ben?" Mack's voice filled with concern.

"Nope. Not at all." He stood, hands on his hips, still clutching the book in one. If someone had told him a month ago that he'd live right next door to the author of the book for the movie he was filming, he'd have thought them crazy.

"Ring me up, would you Mack? I'll take this too." He held up his hand, still holding the book.

CHAPTER 2

She held the paper in her hands, not quite believing it. Since splitting with her husband, ex-husband, she corrected herself, four years ago, NY Times best-selling author, Abbi Peterson was free… free to do what she pleased, when she pleased and who she pleased.

Ha! Like that will ever happen again, she thought with a sad smile. The split had been mutual, but it had come at a price for her. It was only mutual when she had willingly given her ex half of her royalties for the first year. Lucky for him it was being filmed for the big screen. Otherwise, he wouldn't have gotten squat. Towards the end of their relationship, he started squandering her advance cheque. If she had stayed, she was certain… without a doubt, she'd be broke by now. Marrying young after their firstborns, they had grown their separate ways, long before she completed the first draft of her manuscript. She couldn't hate him; he had given her three awesome kids, all adults now… twins, Luke and Lane, 29 and Ava, 27. For that, she'd be eternally grateful. Tossing the letter aside, she opened the cupboard to get the morning underway.

The snap of the can opener was the call of the breakfast bell for her menagerie of pets. Flying into the kitchen in a frenzy of hair, feathers, and dust. Each one of her five dependents held a special place in her heart. She had two dogs. Lucy, her aging cuddle bug Yorkie, and a Bull Mastiff American Bulldog mix, who was so aptly named Brutus. She brought him into the family fold for his intimidating physique after a break-in a few months back. They guaranteed her at the time of rescuing that he'd know that his sole purpose in life was to protect his mistress. He failed miserably at it. With his lopsided grin and lolling tongue forever hanging out, he was the goofiest member of their family. But he was a work in progress. Being a pup of only a year didn't help matters, but he was getting better. He at least now knew the cats, Null and Void were not his toys to drag about and that Bird, a beautiful sulfur-crested cockatoo, could indeed fly around at will. Cussing the blue blazes out of anything he encountered, Bird was the boss of their cozy abode and knew it too.

They kept her company; they kept her sane when living in such a remote area was sometimes terrifying. Terrifying because every little sound had her jumping out of her skin, thinking someone was watching her. After the break-in, things just snowballed for her. She craved her privacy to the point of being considered a recluse, so to speak. Not anything too drastic mind you, she still socialized with the locals, but that was it. She even avoided the web as much as possible, not caring to know what was going on in the world outside her bubble. The closest neighbor was 500 feet away. Well, would be, if anyone was living there.

The house had been vacant that she knew of, for the past three years. When she had purchased her property on the shores of Pearl Lake, she had wanted to purchase it. Her real estate agent, Nigel, told her it wasn't for sale… some Hollywood actor had owned it as a vacation retreat and therefore it would never be on the market. She left Nigel with explicit instructions to let her know the second it came available on the market, as she planned to snag it up. She hated being so secluded, but she also didn't want any hotshot ruining her peace and tranquility.

Abbi just remembered she needed to get to Mackwells, her go-to-spot in the village. She had to pick up some much-needed food and wine. The wine was a must! She had to get back to writing her book, and soon. Her agent had been breathing down her neck to get her second book in her series finished by the deadline, and she had hit a brick wall, she needed to get the gears rolling somehow.

She glided to the library where she turned on Marshall, her self-cleaning vacuum. Yes, she had named her vacuum cleaner. It was the only way to get Bird to leave it alone. Otherwise, he'd swoop down, trying to attack it every time it was running. With it having a name he must have thought it was just another animal she had added to her collection.

Biting her lip, she debated what to do next. Deciding that the windows were next on her agenda, she went into the kitchen. There was a bird's nest above one window, and they had done a fine job of making a mess. From under the sink, she grabbed paper towels and window cleaner and headed out onto the porch.

Standing on a stepladder, Abbi was on her third window when she heard something... *What the hell is that*? She stopped mid swipe of her vigorous scrubbing to get a better listen. *Is that music*? Faintly, she could hear it, but couldn't pinpoint where it was coming from. Rock music... she could tell by the beat.

She peered towards the vacant house. Looking through the trees, she could just see the outline of the roof in the distance. Climbing down from the stepladder, she headed for the steps to get to ground level, tripping on the loose board of the bottom step. Flailing about, she tried unsuccessfully to grab the railing, falling flat on her face. With an "oomph," Abbi pushed herself up, and quickly glanced around to see if anyone saw.

They didn't you fool! There's no one around for miles, she reminded herself, making a mental note to fix that damn step. With a pivot, she marched back towards the house to finish the windows. Just as she was about to set her foot down on the cursed step, she heard laughter and froze... A horrifying realization hit her; someone saw her!

Now she had to get to the village grocers. She just had to find out if there were any newcomers. It was expected any day now. The season was just about to start, and people would flock to her hideaway. She flew up the steps and into the house to take a quick shower.

Letting her wavy hair air dry, Abbi twisted it into a knot, holding it in place with a clip. It had been unseasonably humid for late April. At least her hair wouldn't be a mass of frizz by the time she got to the village. She quickly dressed in a pair of faded blue denim capris, a white t-shirt, and a paisley poncho. She called the dogs to go out for a quick pee, impatiently tapping her foot for them to pick the perfect spot. Finally, they both ambled up the steps and back into the house. She slipped her feet into a pair of white sneakers. Grabbed her purse and cell phone, she kissed each dog. And with a "Be Good, you two," tossed over her shoulder, she set the alarm, pulling the locked door closed behind her. Carefully sidestepping the bottom step, she once again glanced over to the vacant house. Did she dare go over there? No, she'd wait and see what she could find out first before ambling up to a deserted place alone. Besides, Brutus would come with her. He might be a doofus, but he did still protect her when the need arose. She started at a quick jaunt towards the village, getting there in record time.

Removing the clip from her hair, she finger-combed her wavy locks into some sort of order. Pushing the door open to Mackwells, the tinkling bell above the door announced her arrival. Every time she came in, it felt like she catapulted back in time 40 years.

"Hey Mack, how's it going?" Abbi called, walking down the gleaming hardwood floors that creaked with every step.

She sat on a barstool at the lunch counter, thinking she'd grab a quick bite to eat before getting her essentials. She glanced at the daily specials written on the chalkboard on the wall behind the counter, undecided.

"Abbi! Good, good. What can I get you, girl?" She had to smile at that; she was hardly a girl anymore.

"Coffee and a toasted fried egg sandwich, please," she responded.

Setting her coffee cup down in front of her, Mack asked, "So, how are things out at your place, everything quiet?"

Mack was an aging bear of a man. Ever since the break-in, he was like a father to her.

"Yup, it's been really quiet lately. Although I think I heard some music playing earlier this morning," she frowned.

"Well, on calm mornings like this, sound carries around the lake. It's hard to tell where it came from... likely across the water," he said, wiping the counter.

Abbi had never thought of that. She supposed he could be right; she was likely overreacting.

"I'll go get your sandwich ready, be right back," he called over his shoulder as he ambled away.

Looking around the condiment caddy for the cream that wasn't there, Abbi got up, going around the counter to the fridge along the wall, "Hey Mack, I'm just grabbing the cream."

"Sure thing," he yelled, from the kitchen.

She was checking her email when Mack placed a plate in front of her. "Here you go, honey. I'm sorry about that." He motioned at the sugar and cream as he sat her sandwich before her.

Abbi had completely forgotten she even got up to get them. She smiled his concern away with a "thanks" and grabbed the sugar jar, adding just a dash. She exchanged the sugar for the little cream pitcher, intending to just add a splash. Mid-pour, the tinkling of the bell had her glancing around to the entrance to see who was coming in.

Her mouth gaped open, her eyes growing large. A soft, "Oh my!" escaped past her lips... *And who do we have here?* she wondered snapping her jaw closed.

CHAPTER 3

Abbi had never seen the man that just walked into Mackwells. And oh, what a man he was! Tall and broad-shouldered, his dark hair shimmered with blonde highlights. Not dyed, but kissed from the sun, looked tousled as if he was out for a quick jog or had just rolled out of bed. She couldn't figure out which, but the latter brought a pleasant image to her mind. She swallowed hard, not taking her eyes off him. *A man that looks that good has got to be an ass!* ... That didn't stop her from getting her fill.

She heard Mack call out. "Hey. Ben. How are you doing today?"

Hmm... Ben is it? Abbi thought, as she looked between the two men while they exchanged small talk. She noted he had an accent... British if she wasn't mistaken; and oh boy, he was young. Young enough to be her kids' ages. With a dreamy sigh, she thought, *Oh well. God gave eyes to look girl,* and she was a looking!

He glanced her way. "Ah... excuse me, Miss."

MISS? Abbi was sure she was the only woman sitting at the counter. She turned her head to see just who he was talking to. He's talking to me! She whipped her head back around. Suddenly she felt all giddy inside, not ma'am but Miss. Lordy! She felt like a schoolgirl. She was blushing like one too, no doubt! Her heart racing, she smiled. "Yes?"

"You..." he made a sound in his throat while inclining his head, "Err... you're spilling a bit there," he gestured to the counter.

What the hell kind of greeting is that?! Slightly confused, Abbi shook her head. "What?" she asked.

He stood there with a shy grin on his face, gazing intently at the counter. Following his gaze, she saw she was still pouring cream into her coffee. She pulled back with a shocked, "*Oh!*" just as the cream was about to spill onto her lap. Abbi's legs tangled around the stool, tripping her up. Helpless, she felt herself falling backward.

Good Lord! I'm going to fall ass over teakettle in front of a perfect specimen of God's gift to women... albeit a young one, but a perfect one.

She braced for the impact of the floor that never came. Instead, she felt her back encounter a chest of steel. Strong hands lifted her to stand. Somehow her beautiful paisley poncho had a mind of its own, thinking it would be better suited as a hat. The back of it flipped over her head, covering her face. Abbi stood for a moment, not knowing what she should do. What she did know was that at that very moment the floor could open and swallow her whole, and she'd be completely fine with it.

She felt herself being turned around, felt her newly fashioned hat being lifted and flipped back down her back. She fixed her eyes on the floor. A firm, but gentle hand lifted her chin. Abbi had no choice but to look in his searching eyes, eyes filled with genuine concern.

"Are you all right?" she heard him say.

She should have just nodded and kept her mouth shut. But oh no... NOT Abbi Peterson. She said the first thing that popped into her head.

"You smell really good." Mortified, she pivoted on her heel, marching herself to the ladies' room.

Walking to the counter, Ben sat tugging up his sleeves and asked Mack for a coffee. "Ah... I'm curious," he squinted, tilting his head. "Is she always like that?" he asked grinning.

Cleaning the spilled creamer off the counter and floor, Mack chuckled. "Pretty much. Normally, not that bad though." His laughter grew in momentum. "She's a little klutzy from time to time." He was full out belly laughing at this point. "But I never... I've never seen her like that before."

By this time Mack was bent over... smacking his knee, cackling laughter erupted past his lips. "Ooh!" he sucked in a breath. Wiping tears out of his eyes, he walked into the kitchen to retrieve Ben's coffee.

"You *idiot!*" Abbi told her sodden reflection in the mirror over the sink for the tenth time. She splashed more cool water on her face, hoping it would remove the telltale blush from her cheeks. She grabbed a fistful of paper towels, blotting her face dry. Of all the things one could say to a person upon being asked if she were all right, she just had to say... *You smell really good. What the hell is wrong with me?* she thought sourly. She glanced at her watch. Fifteen minutes had gone by since she made her escape to the washroom. With one long last look in the mirror, she turned the doorknob, praying that Ben had left.

Rounding the corner, she spied him sitting at the counter. Stopping in her tracks, she took a deep breath, intent on walking right up to him to apologize and thank him. Instead, she veered off to the pet aisle. Calmly, she selected a few tins of dog and cat food and searched out the birdseed. Grabbing a few boxes of those, she walked to the snack aisle. Bird just loved peanuts in the shell and if she didn't get him those, he'd curse at her for days. Next was a bottle of the bubbly. Abbi selected one, thought better of it and grabbed two more. She'd need it after today. Juggling her findings, she could no longer avoid Ben.

As she headed to the counter to pay, out of the corner of her eye she saw him get up and start walking towards her. Keeping the counter in her sights, she prayed that the third bottle of wine stayed in her firm grip. She could picture it now, the bottle slipping from the death grip she had on it, crashing to the floor. Hopefully, it would just smash but knowing her luck, she'd step on it and off it would carry her like a rolling log on water.

"Hey. Here, let me help you," his deep voice interrupted her thoughts.

Not waiting for a response, he took the items, settled them on the counter and casually leaned against it. He folded his arms across his chest waiting for her. Abbi made her way to it slowly. As she approached, he straightened, taking a step towards her with his hand outstretched.

"I'm sorry. I haven't properly introduced myself," he said as he stared into her eyes.

Abbi had always had an issue making eye contact. She didn't like it. It always made her feel like someone could see her soul and she avoided it at all costs.

"I'm at a slight advantage here. I know your name is Abbi, but you don't know mine. I'm Ben Quinn."

The way her name rolled off his tongue had her weak in the knees. Damn that British accent! Abbi couldn't tell if he was being nice or just plain sexy! *This guy is trouble.* She licked her suddenly dry lips. She couldn't for the life of her look at anything but his eyes.

"Pleased to meet you," Abbi murmured taking his hand. Okay. Now she was being silly. She did not just feel a jolt as if she stuck a fork in a wall plug. Funny thing was, in his eyes, she saw it too. They jerked their hands back just as Mack came ambling up to the pay counter.

"Mack… um… can I… get… ah…." *Jesus, Abbi, spit it out,* her mind screamed. "Get a coffee to go with this, please?" she rushed on, breathlessly.

"Sure thing, Hun. Gotta make a fresh pot. Decaf, right?" Mac called over his shoulder as he went to get it.

She nodded rapidly. "Yes, please."

"So., I guess I'll see you around then," Ben said, looking at her.

"Oh, are you here for the summer?" Abbi asked, slowly recovering from her shock.

"For now," he pursed his lips. "I haven't decided on the long term yet. Will have to look the place over, make sure I can get it ready in time for winter, that is… if I stay. I like the fact that it's so isolated but then it isn't. You know what I mean?"

"I do! That's what drew me to the area myself. The views are spectacular all year round. It's lovely," she enthused. She loved living here.

"I agree with you about that, the spectacular views, that is. They are quite beautiful," he added softly, looking her up and down appreciatively.

Okay…. It's not the accent. Abbi had to bite her lip to contain herself. She turned her head away quickly to stifle a smile. Get a grip girl, she thought, tapping the counter. *He's young enough to be your kid!*

"Mack!" her voice cracked. "You got that coffee ready yet?"

"Yup! Just pouring it now," he returned.

Taking a deep breath, Abbi turned her head back to Ben. "Well, it was nice meeting you, enjoy your stay."

"I'm sure I will, thank you," he responded, a soft smile tugged the corners of his lips as he went back to his waiting coffee.

"So, I see you met Ben. Seems like a nice enough fellow." Mack stated as he rang up her items. "You two seemed to hit it off.
"

"Yes. We did… meet that is." Abbi blushed as she fumbled in her wallet for the cash. She mumbled her apologies as she thrust the bills at him, knowing Mack was always short of coins.

"At least you won't be all alone out there now." He handed her change to her.

"What do you mean by that, Mack?" looking down as she concentrated on stuffing the money in her wallet.

Considering it was just her place and the vacant actor's house… No way! So, he was the actor who owned the house.

"Hmm, well, it's about time he came and did something with the place, letting it sit there to rot away," Abbi responded with a little more annoyance than warranted. *Calm down, it wasn't sold.*

"Oh no, that's not him. No, Ben, bought it from the actor,"

Without moving her head, Abbi glanced up. One brow arched as she looked at Mack, then she turned her attention to Ben, giving him a sidelong glare. Her annoyance turned into rage. Ben must have been watching her, for he gave her a quick smile and a wave of his hand.

She turned her attention back to Mack. "I have to go now," Abbi spoke in a rushed monotone. Grabbing her bags from the counter, she turned on her heel. In the few steps it took to reach the door, she was already cursing out her real estate agent, Nigel. *Just you wait, mister, until I get out of here and tear you a new one!* Shoving the door, she discovered her escape was blocked. No matter how hard she pushed and shoved, the door would not budge. Turning to Mack, she made a desperate sound in the back of her throat.

"Uh, Abbi. You've got to pull the door open, towards you, Hun." he supplied.

She closed her eyes. *How many times must I embarrass myself in front of this man today? At least 5, but who is counting?* came the quick response. Tossing one last heated look behind her before exiting, Abbi shot Ben a quick huff and out the door she went.

Ben barked out a laugh. "She is certainly entertaining, isn't she?"

Mack chortled in response, "That she is, Ben my boy, that she is."

CHAPTER 4

Abbi was fuming mad. As she walked home, she debated stopping to call Nigel and find out what the hell happened. She was close to tears; she was so mad. He knew she was interested in that place and settled for her own. Yes, she had made her house a home over the years, adding her personal touch to it, but that wasn't the point!

To hell with it. She stopped, dropped her bags and fumbled in her purse for her phone. Agitated beyond belief, she scrolled through her contacts until she found Nigel's number. Stabbing his name with her finger felt great... like she was poking him in the eye. He picked up on the fourth ring. "Nigel. Abbi Peterson here," she said testily.

"Abbi, darling! It's so nice to hear from you. What can I help you with?"

"If I recall, I asked you to tell me the *second* the house on the point came up on the market," she bristled.

"Let me just pull your file up here. Okay, let's see," he mumbled to himself, reading the notes.

Her mind strayed to her encounter with Ben. How strong his arms felt, how gentle his touch was on her chin. *Stop it! He's a kid for Pete's sake.* And besides, she was mad at him for buying her house!

"Ah-ha! Here it is. Yes, you said that you would take it the second it came up. Money wasn't an issue and full asking price would be the offer. It's all here, yes!"

"Just what I thought. Can you tell me then why you didn't call me about it?" surprising herself at how calm she was.

"Whatever do you mean, my dear Abbi?" he sounded confused.

Okay, he is lying, or he doesn't have a clue. It had to be the latter. He stood to lose a nice hefty commission on the sale of that place, so he had no reason to lie about it. Now she felt terrible how she talked to him. And especially how she had treated Ben. Drained, as the fight left her, she felt exhausted.

"Never mind Nigel. I'm sorry. I must be mistaken." Her voice trailed off with guilt. She supposed it wouldn't be so bad having someone close by. She just wished they had been old and crotchety instead of, well, Ben.

Pushing that thought to the back of her mind, she picked up her bags and continued home. Ten minutes later she was looking at her house, admiring the three sparkling windows from their earlier scrubbing, making a mental note to finish the rest. That's odd. All her animals were sitting in the bay window, including Bird. In the middle was Brutus, howling his fool head off. *Good Lord, I wasn't long.* She bounded up the steps, fumbling with her keys. Finally, she got it open, and they rushed at her as if they hadn't seen her in days.

She set the bags in the kitchen as the dogs danced around her legs. Lucy, in her quiet demeanor, pawed the air and Brutus yipped with excitement, both communicating their need to go outside. She walked through the living room at the back of the house; the dogs followed close on her heels. She loved this room the most. The massive stone fireplace drew the eye to the room from the kitchen. But once in the living room, the windows that lined the walls gave a view of the lake from all directions. She opened the doors that led out onto the covered back porch. Taking a seat on a lounge chair, she waited for the dogs to finish their business. She glanced at her watch, noting that it was almost dinnertime, her favorite time of day. The sun would soon start its descent, painting the stillness of the lake with its reflection of orange and reds. The loons would soon be out on the lake, too. Their haunting wail echoing, calling to each other, sending shivers along her spine. She loved it.

Cries of a dog in peril interrupted her musings. *Oh, my goodness! Lucy and Brutus!* Panic had her jumping out of her seat. Racing down the steps, she called to them. Her relief was replaced with concern when, with a howl, Brutus responded, standing at the water's edge with Lucy by his side, both staring intently towards the beach across the lake.

Nothing appeared out of the ordinary to Abbi. She peered to the shore across the way. It was deserted, as it always was. As far as she knew it was just vacant land.

Wait... is that someone with a flashlight in the woods? She peered closer. *Must be my imagination or just headlights from the road beyond.* Still, though, something was out there and hurting by the sounds of it. A chill ran along her spine as she turned away. Abbi was tempted to get in her car and search for the injured animal. Knowing the way sound carried across the lake, it would be futile to do so. She could look for days and never find it in the dense trees. With a sad sigh, she called out as she set off for the house. "Come on, guys. Let's get you some food." Both came trotting behind her.

Halfway to the house, Brutus shot past her, a low growl emitting from his throat that turned into crazed barking as he got closer to the house. Someone was on her porch, sitting in the chair she had earlier vacated. "Brutus come!" she ordered. Of course, he didn't listen. She envisioned him attacking whoever it was. Silence descended. She started to run, with Lucy barking at her heels. Reaching the bottom step, she stood there a moment in disbelief. Her watchdog was lying flat out on his back, legs stiff in the air, groaning in pleasure as he was getting the mother of all belly rubs by none other than... Ben. *Lucky dog,* she thought fleetingly. *Damn it, stop that!*

"Hey there, Abbi," he said in his deep accent.

"Hi, I see you've met Brutus," she nodded. "As you can tell, his bark is worse than his bite, and this here is Lucy. She's shy with strangers," she said, glancing down.

"Yeah." He snickered, "He's a tad intimidating. For a minute there I thought I was in for it," he said, crouching down to greet Lucy. Glancing up at Abbi, he said, "I thought I would pop by to see how you're doing."

"I'm fine," she mumbled. Abbi was waiting for Lucy to cower away with her tail tucked tightly between her legs. It shocked her when the tiny dog stayed in one place.

"Hello, Miss Lucy. Now, aren't you a sweet one," he said softly, stretching out a hand for her to sniff. He was granted a small lick and a wag of her tail. She scooted closer to put her tiny paws on Ben's leg to get better leverage and promptly smothered him in kisses.

"Wow. I'm impressed; she likes you," she marveled. "Ever since the break-in, she hides when anyone comes to visit."

Glancing up, Ben sighed. "Right. Mack told me about that. I can only imagine how that must have affected you." Looking down, he added, "And Miss Lucy here. He mentioned she was missing for a day or so?" he questioned, continuing to pet both dogs at the same time while looking up at her.

Abbi wrinkled her brow. She hated thinking about it. "Yes. We… as in me and the police..." *Why did I feel the need to explain that?* "… figured she must have darted out the door when they kicked it in. I thought I lost her for good." She sighed, shaking her head. "I found her two days later, on your porch, huddled in the corner. She was muddy, her hair matted with leaves and sticks." She shivered at the memory.

Ben must have thought she was catching a chill. With one last pet to both dogs, he said, "It's cooling down a bit; I don't want to keep you." Standing up he added, "Oh, I almost forgot. I've brought over a little something for you," he reached beside the chair, producing a bunch of wildflowers.

"Oh!" She felt the blush. "They are beautiful. You didn't have to do that." She reached out to take them, inhaling the scent. She'd never received flowers before for no reason. Come to think of it, not even from her ex.

"There is a field of them just on the other side of my house. I thought you might enjoy them after the day you had," he grinned, stuffing his hands into the pockets of his jeans.

"Please, don't remind me," she said with a laugh, admiring the flowers. "Um, I was just about to get the dogs their dinner. Do you want to come in for a coffee? I mean… you don't have to if you need to be going. I completely understand." She should have just let him take his leave. She didn't want to encourage him. But honestly, she didn't want to be alone after revisiting the memory of the break-in. Not waiting for his answer, Abbi walked through the open doors, the dogs trailing behind her.

"Yeah," he nodded. "I'd like that," he responded with a smile, following the three of them in.

Abbi went directly to the kitchen counter to fetch a vase from under the sink. She busied herself putting water in it, and the kettle. "I only have instant is that okay?" she tossed over her shoulder as she placed it on the stove to boil.

"It's fine it's all I have to drink at my house," Ben responded glancing around.

"Perfect, I'll just get these in some water, then I'll get the animals' food ready." She placed the flowers in the vase and began to arrange them.

Animals? Ben thought. He only saw the two dogs drooling patiently at the mention of food. "If you like, while you do that, I can feed them," he offered.

"Would you? That would be great." She smiled her thanks. "The tins are in the drawer to my left. On the left are the dogs' and the cat tins on the right are for Null and Void." Abbi finished arranging the flowers, walking to the dining table she carefully set them in the middle of it. "There," she softly said, still touched at his thoughtfulness.

Ben squinted his eyes. "Did you just say, 'null and void'?" he asked, not sure if he heard her right.

She put a hand on the table, leaning; she smiled and nodded. "Yeah, I did. When I got them, the contract from the breeder, stated it would be null and void if they were to go outside. Try telling them they have to stay inside."

He laughed. "Did you send a picture of them enjoying the sunshine in the yard?"

"I did! They weren't impressed," she grinned.

She went back to the counter and gathered cups, coffee, and sugar on a tray. She noticed Ben standing at the opened drawer. Smiling at him, she said, "The opener is in there too. They each get one, except Brutus, he gets two. Under the counter, in the big plastic tub, are peanuts in the shell, only one scoop. You'll find all their dishes there, too."

Shut up now Abbi, she told herself. She was babbling and knew it; he didn't need such explicit instructions. But hell, she was nervous! Walking to the fridge for the   cream, she gathered some snack food too. Walking back to the counter she

glanced at him to apologize, but he spoke first.

"Okay, got it. But, um, which one of them gets the peanuts?" he inquired with a puzzled look.

He looked so confused she couldn't help but laugh at him, "I'm so sorry, I kinda rattled it off to you, didn't I?" She placed the food on the counter and started to arrange

it in neat stacks on a plate, she dumped a generous heap of crackers in the middle.

"Yeah… a bit," he chuckled. He scooped the contents into the bowls. With a flourish, he presented the dogs with their dinner along with a scratch on their heads. "Why, hello there, you beautiful beast," he marveled.

For a second, Abbi thought he was talking to her. She didn't think of herself as a beast, though. Until she heard the "meah" only Null could create. "That would be Null. And you're right he is a beast." He was a beautiful long-haired, gigantic cat and jet black, larger than Lucy, but gentle as a kitten. "… and that is Void," she motioned, as he waddled his way to his food dish. He was smaller than Null, identical in every way, but solid with short, stubby legs. She explained how the cat couldn't hear for the life of him, having been born deaf. The kettle began its shrill whistle. "Oh! Almost forgot… the peanuts are for Bird," she said, as she turned it off.

Bird? Ben cocked his head. What the hell was that shrill? He watched Abbi shut the kettle off, so he knew that wasn't it.

"Oh, shit! Hit the deck!" Abbi yelled, motioning with her hands for him to get down.

"What… why?" *Was she off her meds?* he thought fleetingly before he noticed the shrill was a shriek. It was louder now, followed by, "Asshole! Get out of my house!"

No time to waste. Ben dropped to the floor, just as the bird swooped to where he had stood a second before. He glanced up from his spot on the floor as a huge slobbery tongue swiped across his face. Brutus grinned at him with complete adoration. Laughing, Ben rolled onto his back, scratching Brutus on the belly while they both watched Abbi take after his attacker.

"Bird! You get in your cage! Now!" Abbi yelled, clapping her hands as she chased Bird around the house. When that didn't get the result she wanted, she started flapping her arms about as if she was the one trying to take flight.

"Piss off!" Was the response she got as Bird cackled about the room.

Grabbing a scoop of peanuts, she called sweetly, heading to the library and his cage. "Oh look, Bird! Look what I have for you!" She shook the scoop as she dumped the contents into his dish. Standing beside it, she waited as he landed on top of the cage. He swung down by his beak, landing on his perch inside.

Promptly she closed the door as he squawked innocently, "love you."

Sure, you do, you bastard, she thought with a shake of her head.

Instead, she replied, "Yeah, yeah. I love you too, asshole."

She rushed back into the kitchen to see Ben still lying on the floor, eyes closed and shaking. *Oh, my goodness! Did he hit his head?*

She knelt at his side. "Ben?" She called out softly, nudging his chest. His hand snaked out grasping her wrist. He pulled her towards him as he opened his laughing eyes.

"Please, join me down here," he said, tugging her closer as he laughed uncontrollably. "I dare say, you have a... err... lovely ceiling." His laughter was contagious as she joined him, feeling him tuck her at his side. "Here," he said, putting an arm out to cushion her head. Their laughter finally calming to an occasional chuckle.

"Ah Man. That felt great! I needed that Abbi. Thank you for that." He glanced at her, searching her face for a reaction. "I have to say, I've met a lot of women in my line of work, but never one as remarkable as you," he mumbled, gazing into her eyes.

She knew that look; he was going to kiss her! Should she let him? *No, Abbi, you can't let him do that!* But a part of her wanted him to. She wanted to throw caution to the wind and to hell with what was right or wrong. For once in her life, she just wanted the moment to happen and not analyze it. She watched as he came closer, inch by inch. Closing her eyes for fear of them going crossed, she waited for the moment their lips met.

She felt the lightest brush on her... forehead? *What the hell was that?* Her eyes snapped open meeting his. Was that... desire she saw in them?

"Please, forgive me. But I've wanted to do this since the minute I saw you." He gently grabbed her jaw. Guiding her face towards him, holding it as if it was a lifeline. Their lips met... softly, like the touch of a feather... tenderly seeking. A shriek from Bird brought Abbi to her senses. Breaking off the kiss, she grabbed his hand that still held her face. She rested her forehead on his, catching her breath. She didn't know what to say to break the silence. Ben did so for her.

"How about that coffee now?" He murmured.

Good, God! His voice just then almost had her jumping his bones. Instead, she broke out into a grin, replying, "Yes, that sounds wonderful."

They sat out on the back porch with their drinks in hand. The plate of food on the table between them, both dogs lying at their feet. Neither one mentioned the kiss, and for that Abbi was thankful. It was bad enough that she couldn't stop thinking about it, but it would have been terrible if he mentioned it. That was something she needed to process in her mind.

"So, the other day, when I was at Mack's, he mentioned that you're a writer. I bought a copy of your book." He paused, selecting some cheese and kielbasa, stacking them on a cracker. Taking a bite, he chewed thoughtfully. "I have to say, I'm impressed with the writing. You did very well for it being your first," he remarked.

Blowing on her steaming coffee, she nodded in agreement. "Thanks. I am surprised myself. I started it after my daughter moved out. Empty nest syndrome got to me… just a tad." She laughed at the memory.

"Good, for you. Well, not the empty nest part," he stated. "It explains why it's so dark!"

"It wasn't easy. What, with my marriage crumbling and work, it was hard to find the time, but I'm happy I did."

She was happy. Something she hadn't been in a long time. She had almost forgotten what it felt like. "As for it being dark, it was a dark time in my life. I guess you could say I poured my heart into that book."

She took a celery stick from the plate. Swirling it in the dip, she popped the end in her mouth, biting it off. Chewing, she said, "I love this time of day. Have you heard them yet?" She asked, motioning towards the lake with the celery.

Bringing a stacked cracker to his mouth to take a bite, he stopped midway. "Pardon?" He said. "Heard who?"

A haunting wail came across the lake. It was just about dusk, the sun almost hidden from sight. "Bloody hell! What was that?"

She looked over at him with a grin. Ben hadn't heard the loons yet, clearly. She smiled. "That my friend is a loon. Listen, you'll soon hear its mate."

She watched the play of emotions cross his handsome face.

"That is so hauntingly beautiful," he remarked in amazement.

"Isn't it though! The first time I heard them, it brought tears to my eyes. They sounded so sad."

"Do they do that all the time?"

"Sadly no. Only from mid-May to mid-June usually. They're early this year," she replied munching on a carrot stick.

They fell silent, just sitting, listening to the marvel of Mother Nature.

Darkness soon fell. Ben held out his hand. "Abbi?"

Shyly, she reached for it, feeling the warmth radiate from him as he rubbed the back of her hand with his thumb. Tonight, she had stepped out of her comfort zone. She had thrown caution to the wind and just lived for the moment. Tomorrow was another day, another day to do the right thing, the proper thing. But tonight, there they sat, hand in hand, listening to the haunting songs of the loon.

CHAPTER 5

Ben awoke to sunlight streaming across his face. *I really ought to get some window coverings* he thought, as he reached for his cell on the bedside table. He squinted, trying to focus on the time… 6:58 am. He groaned as he noticed the exuberant amount of notifications on his social media accounts. He left it on the table, face down. He didn't want to deal with that right now. Stretching the kinks out of his neck and back, he clasped his hands behind his head. He thought about going back to sleep, but with that sunlight, he couldn't. His mind wandered to thoughts of Abbi like it did every day… all day, since he met her. It had been almost two weeks since he last saw her.

His lips broke out into a smile at the thought of her. She was remarkable. She was shy; he had noticed from the start. But as well she was sweet, caring, smart, and funny as hell. She had him in stitches without even trying. She was a tad klutzy. He laughed, thinking about the first day they met at Mack's place. It felt like he had known her for years. But most importantly, she was real. She let her natural beauty shine through without even realizing it. Unlike the women he had met in his chaotic life… the fake ones, the ones that were only trying to hook their claws into someone in his position. She hadn't even asked him what he did for a living, nor did he offer.

With a sigh, he glanced towards the window, looking at the trees beyond. His expression softened. No, she was nothing like that. She was a breath of fresh air. She was special. He thought about the kiss. Never in his life had he kissed a woman on the first day of meeting her. It was like he was drowning, and her mouth was his only lifeline. The only way to describe the feeling was a need. He needed to taste her lips, to feel them under his own. It scared the hell out of him. To be honest, she scared the hell out of him. The way she made him feel so alive was something he realized he hadn't felt in a very long time. He wanted to get to know her better if she'd let him. He wondered if she'd go with him shopping to get something to cover the window.

On that thought, he tossed the covers aside and threw his legs over the side of the bed. Standing there naked with the sun shining on his body. *Yup, need to cover that window for sure!* All he needed was the paparazzi finding out where he lived. He and his peace and quiet would be gone in a heartbeat.

Abbi stepped out of the shower, she groped blindly for a towel hanging on
the rack. Leaving the bathroom, she went to get dressed.
Taking a quick look out the
window, she figured it would be a repeat of yesterday, another sunny, beautiful day. Dressing in jeans and an old plaid work shirt, she headed to the kitchen for a cup of coffee.

"Good morning my lovelies," she called out to her brood. A stampede of paws broke the silence as she turned to ready their food. Setting their dishes before them, she took some feed to Bird. He squawked his displeasure of being locked in all night. "I'm sorry. How could I forget to let you out again?" She crooned to him opening his door. She knew exactly how she could forget… Ben.

Ever since meeting him, her mind was in a fog. It was a wonder she remembered to do anything. Two weeks had passed since the night he had shown up. After they sat listening to the loons, they had talked about their lives. She told him about her kids, her divorce and what she had done with her life until this point. He talked about his parents and growing up in England. She was disappointed when he said he should be going. She walked him through the house to the front door and stood on the porch to say goodnight. They both reached out the same time for a hug and she didn't want to let him go when he'd brushed his lips against hers. It felt good just being held. Letting him go felt like he took a piece of her with him. She had sat down on the top step watching him go, sitting in the moonlight long after he'd gone home.

With her fingers to her lips, she remembered what it felt like when he kissed her. Even now it made her blush, and her stomach tingle. Strange, she had never felt that way before, not even with her husband when they started dating. Shaking her head to clear her thoughts, she picked up the animals' dishes and placed them in the dishwasher.

Tugging on a pair of garden gloves, she called as she went out the door. "Lucy... Brutus, you two coming?" The dogs took off running across the yard as she made a beeline to the garden shed. Opening the door, she stood in disbelief. *Why did I leave it in this condition?*

"Hey, boy. How are you doing today?" Ben asked as he stroked the dog's head. "And just where is your mistress?" he questioned, looking into the wise eyes.

He knocked on the door, but there was no answer. He thought it odd for her to leave without letting Brutus in. A tiny woof announcing Lucy's arrival had him looking to the side of the house.

"She's out back, is she?" He bounded down the steps, Brutus by his side. Following the dogs, he made his way to the backyard. He glanced at the chairs that Abbi and he sat in and found them empty. He scanned the deserted yard. Where the heck is, she? Calling out her name, he didn't get a response. He started off to the water's edge, thinking something had happened to her. He was just about to pass the garden shed when a missile was launched in his direction.

"Whoa!" he ducked, narrowly being hit by a… life preserver?

Abbi jumped, dropping a shovel with a clatter. "Sweet *baby* Jesus! You scared the crap out of me!" she yelled.

Ben laughed. "Sorry about that. I wasn't expecting projectiles coming out of the shed." Bending, he picked up the preserver. "What are you doing with all of this stuff?" he asked gesturing at the ground.

"Well, I intended on cleaning out the flowerbeds today and came in looking for a rake." She motioned with her hand at the floor. "I found this mess. I have yet to find the rake."

For the first time since his arrival, she glanced at him. *How do you look so damn good first thing in the morning?*

"Do you want a drink or something?" she asked, licking her lips. His eyes immediately went to her mouth.

"Um…" Ben cleared his throat. "Any chance there is a larger town nearby?"

"There is, yes."

Abbi took the preserver from him and hung it on a nail. Ben started gathering empty planters where she had tossed them on the ground and brought them into the shed, stacking them neatly against the wall.

The earthy, woodsy scent of his cologne had her closing her eyes, recalling what it felt like to have his arms around her, his hand caressing her face as he kissed her. She needed to get out of there… Now. Before she did something stupid. Like, sniff him as the dogs did. While his back was turned, she darted out the door.

"What did you have in mind?" she questioned, taking off her gloves.

Glancing around to where she was last standing, he did a full circle before he spied her outside the shed. With a grin, he replied, "Actually. I was wondering if you would go shopping with me… grab some lunch if you like. I'll do the driving if you will be my navigator."

She hesitated. Her mind was already calculating the time it

would take to get to Springbank and back. *That would mean a 45-minute drive one way... sitting near him.*

No more than five hours, she figured. Could she do it? Despite the feelings she had

when she was around him, it was not to go any further. She had already decided that.

She needed to distance herself from him. She was getting attached and fast, which was something she couldn't allow.

"What is it you need? Maybe Mack has it in stock," she offered as a solution.

"I checked there, and he doesn't carry the size I need," he stated.

Her brows shot up in surprise. She nodded her head. The faster she did, the higher her eyebrows rose. "Oh!" she said, a small gasp escaping past her lips.

Ben shot out a bark of laughter, "Blinds, Abbi! I need blinds or curtains for my bedroom. The sun is so brilliant in the morning and I find I rather enjoy sleeping past 6 am. Plus, I sleep naked. Who knows who is out there," he casually said. Lowering his voice to a murmur, he added, "... someone could be watching me." He grinned when he saw the blush rise on her face.

"Nope! You're right. Mack doesn't have those, that's for sure!" She shook her head to clear her thoughts. "Okay. Um... let me change and we can go." She turned to call the dogs as she headed towards the house.

Catching her hand, Ben turned her around to look at him.

God WHY is he so flipping handsome? she thought as she scanned his features.

Why couldn't he be older?

"Honestly, you look perfect just the way you are," he murmured, gazing into her eyes.

"That's sweet of you to say, Ben. But I need to get out of these dusty clothes," she said, wiping her sweaty palms on her pants.

He brushed her cheek with the back of his hand. "You have a

bit of smudge here," he mumbled.

Okay. Abbi, haul ass. Before you jump him. She broke eye contact and backed slowly away.

"Right, I'll just run and get my car. Be back in five minutes," he told her, sprinting off.

CHAPTER 6

Ben sat in the car waiting for Abbi to emerge from the house. Checking his email, he opened one from the director of the film he was working on.

Hey Ben, hope all is well with you and you're enjoying your time off. Just wanted to let you know, filming is pushed back. Won't need you for a bit. It will probably be another month or more before we get set to shoot your scenes. Because of the torrential downpours of late, we need to wait for some dryer conditions here before we get back up and running. Will be in touch, Tony.

He wasn't disappointed. Normally he'd be itching to get back to filming. The break from it all was agreeing with him, he had to admit.

A flash of color caught Ben's eye. Looking up, he saw Abbi coming down the steps of her house. His breath caught at the sight of her. Her hair was down, soft and wavy, falling below her shoulders and bouncing with each step she took. He opened his door, got out, and met her halfway down the walk. Taking her hand, he guided her to the passenger side and opened the door.

"My lady, your chariot awaits," he bowed, as she plopped down on the seat, buckling her belt.

She giggled to herself. *My lady? Oh, I like the sound of that; Stop that Abbi!* Wiping the grin off her face she looked up at him she said, "You didn't need to do that... open my door, I mean."

"I know, but I wanted to." He smiled, looking down at her.

41

Closing the door with a soft thud, he came around and settled himself behind the wheel, snapping his seat belt in place. Starting the car, he looked over to her questioningly as he backed out onto the road, "So, where are we off to?"

"Oh right, I completely forgot you don't know your way around. Do you have GPS? I can just punch it in if you like," she offered. Nodding at her, he smiled and asked, "So, this road takes us around the lake does it?"

"Yes. Just after this bend, we should be right across from my place," she responded. Glancing out at the scenery as it streamed past, Abbi was content sitting in the warm sunshine. She felt like she could take a nap. Feeling her head nod off, she jerked herself awake.

"Hey there sleepyhead," she heard Ben say.

Turning to look at him, with sleepy eyes she mumbled, "Sorry, I think I nodded off for a second."

He glanced at her for a moment before looking back to the road. "Yeah, you did," he chuckled, "for about half an hour."

Her eyes grew large. "No way." she said in disbelief. "I hate falling asleep in a car. If there's going to be an accident, I want to be awake."

She noticed her mouth felt weird. Touching the corner with her fingers, it horrified her to know that she had drooled while she took her little nap. Thankfully, it was on the opposite side of Ben. Using the water bottle, she always had on hand, she took a tissue from her purse, wet it, and wiped her mouth. She noticed Ben looking at her with a raised brow as she vigorously wiped the dried spittle.

"Oh, this." She held up the tissue with a nervous laugh. "Um, I need to wake up. This always does the trick," she made the excuse, groaning inward as she wiped her entire face. Stuffing the tissue in her purse, she leaned back in her seat, taking a swig of her water. Staring at his hands on the steering wheel, she noted how tanned and strong they looked. Yet... so gentle. She remembered his touch, causing her to squirm in her seat. Heaven help her... she felt like an antsy child on a long car ride.

"Do you need to make a pit stop Abbi?" he asked, looking over at her.

She whipped her head to face him.

"What... why?" she blushed knowing he saw her squirm.

"You just seem a bit... agitated," he said. "I thought maybe you needed a rest... or something." He didn't want to come out and say perhaps she needed to use a restroom.

Looking at his profile, she replied, "No. No. I'm good."

He reminded her of a Greek god, one from the movies, not the statues, she thought with a silent snicker. Her eyes were drawn to his lips... so soft, she remembered. His chin and jawline were strong and chiseled. His nose was perfect, a bit of a flare at the nostrils, she noted; dancing, green eyes that sparkled when he was excited. His forehead... wait. She just noticed the ball cap that he was sporting. *He wasn't wearing that when we left?* She wrinkled her brow in thought.

He could feel her eyes upon him, studying him. He rather liked it. Not wanting to break her perusal of him, he remained silent.

"Um, where did the hat come from?" Abbi asked pointing to his head.

"This?" he pointed to it, glancing at her. "Ah... yeah, I put it on while you were napping," he said.

"Oh, okay." she nodded, thinking it odd.

"So, what did you say you do for a living again?" she asked, changing the subject. She saw Ben's hands tense on the steering wheel. *Did I touch a nerve? Wait... am I in a car with my stalker?* she thought in a moment of panic. Ever since her book shot to number one, she had someone constantly messaging her. At first, she responded. She enjoyed interacting with her readers but soon had to stop. The kind messages had turned threatening. The very reason she had moved to such a remote place was that they started sending packages to her home address, not through her book agent. Did he find me? No, surely to God she would know… wouldn't she?

"I uh… I didn't," he cleared his throat. "… say that is…" he paused.

Should he tell her? It wasn't that big of a deal. But he liked her too much for her to treat him differently when she found out.

"Okay…?" she trailed off, darting her gaze out the window. If he was the one, how would anyone ever find her body in the middle of all these trees? She was a goner for sure.

Ben noticed the change in her. *Is that anxiety, I detect, or nervousness? Maybe she does need to use a washroom this time?*

Removing his right hand from the steering wheel, he reached to take her hand and felt her startled jump. A quick glance at her face and he noticed something was wrong. "Hey, are you okay?" he asked, concern filling his voice. He pulled off to the side of the road. Shifting the car into park, he killed the engine and said, "Abbi, look at me." He carefully reached out, turning her face towards him. He saw the tears forming in her eyes. Fear stared back at him. Ben dropped his hand, worried about scaring her more.

"Tell me what's wrong, please," he begged, with anxious concern rising in his voice.

She immediately fixed her eyes on her hands. He looked down at her lap, noting her clenched tight fists.

"If I tell you what I do for a living, will you promise to tell me what's wrong?" he asked.

At her nod, he said, "Okay, but first, I have something else to say… the real reason I haven't mentioned to you what my day job is. Will you promise to listen without interrupting me? And after considerable consideration, weighing all the pros and cons, give me an answer?" he asked.

Intrigued now, she replied, "Yes, I promise," in a small voice. The anxiety was still very real.

Unbuckling his seat belt, he turned towards her in his seat. He wished she'd do the same. He so desperately wanted to reach out to turn her towards himself, but he didn't dare touch her any more than he already had. He could see her jumping out of the car if he tried to do so. Instead, he asked her, "Will you look at me, please?"

She half-turned in her seat towards him, eyes fixed out his window, past his shoulder.

Better than looking at her hands, he thought. With a sigh, he began. "Right. Well, the real reason I haven't told you what my job is

is that I don't want your opinion of me to change. I didn't want you to treat me... differently," he mumbled.

Her mind raced. *What kind of work could he possibly do that would make me do that?* Glancing at him now, she watched his features change with worry... a hitman or a... porn star? *Yup, likely the latter.*

Taking a deep breath, he continued. "Abbi, I like you. I think... or hope you feel the same about me." He glanced up through his lashes to see her reaction. "What I feel when I'm with you...."

Nope, not gonna happen. She shook her head. Just as she was about to state those very words, he held up a hand.

"Please, you promised to hear me out," he reminded her.

"Sorry," she mumbled, crossing her arms on her chest.

"I've never felt this way about anyone before... ever. I want to see where this will take us... if you'll let it."

She noticed it wasn't a question but a statement. She knew she promised to wait, but she just had to say something. "I'm flattered. Really, I am. But don't you think I'm a bit too old for you? I mean, I don't even know how old you are, other than you're close to my kids' ages. You're young and yes..." she nodded her head vigorously, "... I admit, very attractive, but don't you want someone your age? Or do you even know what you want?" she asked.

"I'm thirty-three, I'm not one of your kids. I'm a man and yes, I

45

most definitely know what I want and that is you," he breathed, looking deep into her eyes.

She couldn't help but snort out a laugh. He was so serious! Warning bells went off, as Ava's laughing voice echoed in her mind, *'Watch out for those gigolos, ma. They will be after your money!'* With the sudden flash of anger, she realized there was only one reason he could want her, and that was her money… Ava was right. He was a gigolo, a gold-digging gigolo.

Now, what is wrong with her? Ben inwardly groaned as he noted the anger in her gray eyes. "Look," he said, taking her hand in both of his. "Age makes no difference to me. My mum is ten years older than my dad, if that makes you feel better," he offered.

Her brows shot up. *That would make sense. Why would it bother him when he grew up with it?* "Well, honestly it does, a bit," she admitted.

Biting his lip, he kept the sudden grin from appearing too triumphant.

Oh my! She averted her eyes quickly. He wasn't helping when he looked at her that way. She felt a quick tightness where she had no business feeling! She couldn't let him gloat like that. "I said a bit," she stated, crossing her legs to make the sensation go away. It was not working dammit! Pausing, to do the math she added, "But I'm still older than you by two more years than your parents." She felt the need to point that out.

"Aargh… *Woman…* I don't care!" He threw his hands up in frustration.

Giving him a sidelong glance, she sighed. "Well, maybe I do! I can't promise you anything, but I will think about it. I'll think about us… I mean, you… and me that is," she stated.

"Okay, so tell me about your job?" This shall be good!

With more confidence than he felt earlier, he simply stated, "I'm an actor. Currently, production is shut down for at least a month and a half because of torrential downpours," he recited

Tony's email. He watched her for a reaction.

She was shaking. Was she cold? He realized that wasn't the case when the shaking turned into bubbly laughter. "Ooh, that's a good one, Ben! I must give you an 'A' for effort. Honestly, you don't have to lie. I know you're a gigolo and only after my money." She burst into a fit of laughter.

"Wait… *What?* You think I'm a gigolo? How?" he asked in astonishment, a smile tugging at his lips.

"Well, yeah, because it's the only explanation I could think of why you would want to be with me," she said, wiping away her tears from laughing.

"Abbi, honestly… I'm not lying. As a matter of fact, the movie I'm filming, in which I have the leading role, is 'The Jasper Killings'."

The look on her face was priceless to Ben. He quickly coughed to cover the chuckle that was about to burst forth from his lips as he buckled his seat belt.

"Right then… shall we be off?" Tossing a grin her way, he started the car, put it into gear and drove off.

CHAPTER 7

Abbi's mind raced with his admission.

"It just can't be," she finally recovered. "Your name was not on my list of actors."

Glancing over, Ben noticed the bewilderment on her face. Approaching the city, he kept his eyes on the road. "Tell me something, Abbi. What name was on the list for the leading male?"

Rummaging in her purse, she found her cell phone. Opening her email, she searched for the director's name mumbling, "Tony" repeatedly, as she scrolled through countless messages.

"Sullivan," Ben supplied, just as her eyes found his name.

Glancing at him, she told herself anyone could know the director's name. She opened the email and read it to him.

Hello Abbi, Tony here, I have the list of actors I think would be perfect to do your story, The Jasper Killings. Please let me know if they are acceptable to you.

Detective Sue Martin- Joy Summers

Detective Ethan Fields- Ben Everett

Captain James- John Page

She, of course, had approved without bothering to look the actors up.

Stopping at a red light, Ben interrupted her recitation of names. "Abbi, tell me something." He paused looking over at her. "What name do you use to write under... your pen name, I believe it's called?"

"Abbi Stevens," she supplied. "What does that have to do with this?" she gestured with her phone.

A honk from behind had Ben looking up to the rear-view mirror, noting the finger that was being waved in his direction.

Stepping on the gas, he stated off-topic, "I thought all Canadians were polite." Signaling to turn into the mall parking lot, he continued. "Anyway, back to your question. It has everything to do with your list there."

Parking the car and turning the engine off, he turned in his seat, inching closer to her. Her eyes were drawn to his. His lips mesmerized her as he drew closer, his tongue darting out to wet them. His mouth was now a breath away from hers. She closed her eyes, waiting for the touch of his kiss. "It's simple, really. I don't use my real name for business purposes either," Ben murmured. She could feel the warmth of his mouth so close to hers.

Suddenly air rushed in place of his heat. She heard the soft thump of the door and sprang her eyes open. "Ooh! That man is impossible!" she yelled, stamping her feet on the floor in frustration. *That was so unfair of him to leave me hanging like that!*

Coming around to Abbi's side of the car, he could hear her going off, which made him quite satisfied. Ben smiled sweetly at her as he opened her door, offering his hand to help her out of the car. "Shall we grab something to eat first before we shop?" he suggested.

"Fine by me," she retorted as she took his hand.

He had so badly wanted to kiss her, but he didn't want to pressure her. He hadn't planned on teasing her like that, but it was a spur-of-the-moment

decision. He didn't know if he could stop if he started. Shutting the door, he set the alarm and off they went inside.

Not wanting to show him how hot and bothered she was by that little stunt, she cheerfully said, "I know a great little restaurant, shall we go there?"

"Absolutely," he responded, offering her his arm. "Lead the way," he said, smiling as she took it.

Finding a booth, they slid in opposite sides across from each other. The waitress was a young pretty redhead named Katie, according to the tag on her shirt. She brought them menus and glasses of water.

"Do you two want anything to drink?" Katie asked.

"Water's good for me," Abbi responded.

Katie placed a hand on Ben's shoulder. Abbi caught the quick flash of annoyance as he leaned back in his seat, breaking contact.

"Tea, please," he answered politely.

Did the girl recognize him? Abbi suddenly felt sympathy for him as he sat there, looking at the menu. No wonder he put the hat on.

"Hey," she leaned forward, reaching for his hand. "You okay?" she asked, searching his face.

He glanced up, a smile breaking on his face. "Yeah, I am now." He winked at her as he turned his hand over to hold hers.

"How about we split an order of poutine?" she asked, with a grin.

"That doesn't sound very appealing."

"I promise you; you won't regret it."

"Whatever you want sounds good to me." His eyes twinkled as he stroked the back of her hand with his thumb.

Katie returned to take their order. Looking at Ben, she gave him a dazzling smile. "Are you ready to order?" she asked.

Ben glanced up at her. "Yes, actually... we will share a.... what was it again?" He turned his head towards Abbi with a quizzical look and met a blank stare.

Abbi was too busy concentrating on the sensations his thumb made, stroking the back of her hand. He enchanted her, made her insides melt with just the sound of his voice. She resisted the urge to launch herself across the table.

"*Abbi!*" Ben tugged at her hand, snapping her back to reality.

She saw him looking at her. His brows raised in a questioning look.

"*What?*" she asked, a little too loudly.

He snickered softly, asking again what they had decided.

"Oh! Poutine," replying, as she looked at Katie with a smile.

"Perfect. I'll get right on that," Katie responded with a fake smile as she walked away.

Abbi had to let go of his hand; she couldn't concentrate otherwise. She took a sip of her water. "Can I ask you a question, Ben, and you answer me truthfully?"

"Absolutely. You can ask me anything."

"When we were in the car having our little roadside chat, you said you didn't want my opinion of you to change. Why is that?" Needing a distraction, she grabbed the dessert menu from behind the salt and pepper shakers, scanning it with indifference.

"Usually a handful of people I meet, change their whole demeanor towards me when they find out who I am," he sighed, leaning back in his seat. "Normally, it doesn't bother me, sometimes it's useful, I will admit," he said with a chuckle.

"Fair enough," she nodded. "So," she paused. "Um, does that happen often when you meet… women?" she asked, turning her attention to straightening her utensils.

She didn't want to know how many past lovers he had… more than she cared to know; she bet. No, that would be a major turnoff.

Ben noticed how she avoided looking at him. "Well, most women know who I am, or they soon figure it out. Either way, they are only after one or two things… sex or money. I stay clear of them… usually."

Her head snapped up, one brow arching, their eyes met. He grinned at her.

"I thought that would get your attention," his eyes danced.

"Hey, it's not my business how many…" she gestured with her hand. For the life of her, she didn't know what word to use. *Floozies, flakes, tramps?* "… f… flings, you've had," she stammered out.

"Abbi, when I was in my teens, I had the usual one or two-

51

month relationship, but never anything serious. My last one was six years. We started dating before the fame hit."

He could tell she was mentally counting the years. "I found out she had been seeing someone behind my back. I was off shooting a short film when it happened. She begged me to work it out. I refused. Shortly after, we went our separate ways and three years later I made it in Hollywood," he trailed off.

Finding out he had been cheated on was a blow which he didn't think he could recover from. That's when he threw himself into his work.

"You mean to tell me she cheated on you?" *Was she nuts?*

Katie brought their food. "Here you go, guys." She sat the plate in the middle of the table. Handing Ben a napkin with a longing look, she said, "If there is anything, and I mean anything you need, just call me."

Abbi needed him to continue telling her what happened, he wouldn't do that with Katie standing there. "Yup! We're good, thank you, Katie!" Abbi called out. *Get on your way before I kick you...*

With a huff, Katie gave her a rude look before walking away.

Ben pointed to the plate. "What in the world is this concoction?" he asked in wonderment.

"It's a delectable dish of French fries; chips for you Britt's... topped with cheese curds and smothered in gravy." She grinned, popping a forkful into her mouth.

Picking up his fork, he took a stab at the plate, unsure if he was brave enough to try it. He went for it.

Abbi watched his face for a reaction. Oh, yeah! There it was the look of one who just tasted a little piece of heaven on earth. "You like?" she asked.

"*Wow!*" he blinked rapidly. Taking a few more mouthfuls he picked up the napkin Katie left, wiping his mouth before answering Abbi's question. "This is amazing!"

"What's that?" she asked, pointing to the napkin.

"Did I miss something?" Thinking he had gravy on his chin, he gave it a wipe.

"No, not your face, it's perfect... I mean perfectly clean," she recovered quickly. "I meant on the napkin."

Ben turned it over to where she was looking. Frowning, he smoothed it out. Making a sound of disgust, he showed it to Abbi.

Anger filled her at the Katie's audacity. For her to write that Ben could find a better woman was one thing; Abbi couldn't argue with that, but to leave her phone number too?! "Why that calculating little witch!" Anger was rising with each word. "I'm leaving them a bad review on their website," she said indignantly, whipping out her cell phone.

"Abbi." Ben put his hand on her arm. "It's fine. I'm used to it. It's not the restaurant's fault."

"You're right, but it's still not fair for her to try to pick you up either." God, no wonder he wanted to escape if this was the norm.

"Let's just finish up and get out of here?" he suggested.

She nodded in agreement.

"And to answer your question from earlier..." he paused.

Thank you, baby Jesus.

"Yes, my ex cheated on me. Had been for some time. Three years later, it made me the man I am today," he murmured. Taking her hand in his, he turned it up, placing a soft kiss on her palm then her wrist. A soft groan escaped past her lips. She saw the desire spring to his eyes.

"And I've been celibate ever since."

"Let's leave now, shall we?" she suggested.

Taking his wallet out, he placed a couple of twenties on the table.

Abbi had one more thing to do, taking a pen out of her purse she wrote *Back off... He's taken!* On the napkin. She didn't mean it, sort of. But Katie didn't need to know that! She looked at Ben, swallowing hard as she gestured to the napkin, feeling the need to explain, "Um, well... you know... not *yet!*"

Standing with a huge grin, he held out his hand. "Shall we?" he asked. Nodding, she returned a smile, as she reached for the hand he   offered.

CHAPTER 8

Walking hand in hand through the mall, they headed to the nearest department store.

Abbi caught the glances thrown their way as they went down the main aisle to the housewares department. All the women, young and old, glanced at Ben. She looked at him out of the corner of her eye, just to see if he noticed. He was oblivious to it. The self-doubt she had been feeling all along reared its ugly head once again. *Who am I kidding?* She couldn't possibly entertain a relationship with him. Knowing she was old enough to be his mother; he'd find someone youthful, more attractive. She swallowed at the sting that suddenly appeared in her throat, rapidly blinking the tears away that were forming in her eyes. No, this can't happen, she decided, reluctantly letting go of his hand.

When he looked at her, she pasted a cheerful smile on her lips and bounded towards the blinds. "What color were you thinking of?" she asked.

When he went to put an arm around her waist, she sidestepped away to the curtains. The tears were there again, dammit. *I need to escape, but where?* She grabbed the closest thing to her.

"Would you rather some room darkening drapes?" Thrusting them in his directions, she blocked him from seeing her face. "Here, see what you think," she said, wiping her cheeks.

Something is off with her. Taking the curtains by the bottom, he pulled them down, along with her hand. Noticing the trail of tears on her cheeks, he took her face in his hands. Wiping them away with his thumbs, he asked softly, "Abbi, what's wrong?"

"Uh, nothing… nothing at all. I just have something in my eyes," she quietly stated, dashing them away again.

His brows shot up. "Both of them?" not believing her for a second.

"Yeah… both of them," she replied sadly.

His heart went out to her. Clearly, something was wrong. Whatever it was, her tears tore him up inside. Enveloping her in his arms, he held her, stroking her hair. He could feel her body wracking, with silent sobs. "It's okay," he whispered against her ear. "Whatever it is, we will work it out together."

She broke away from his embrace. Shaking her head, no longer being able to endure his kindness. *He just doesn't understand and likely never will.* Taking a deep breath, she gave him a watery smile.

Looking at the wrinkled curtains clutched in her hands, he chuckled. "I guess these are as good as any."

"Oh," she sniffed. "I'm sorry. I didn't realize I still had them. I'll pay for them." she offered.

"It's fine. I rather like black anyway. Come on, let's get home. You have your pets waiting for you."

Giving a nod, she allowed him to guide her to the checkout. Halfway there, Abbi noticed a stunning young blonde making a beeline for Ben… one of the same girls eyeballing him earlier. No doubt she was making laps around the store in search of him.

"Excuse me, but aren't you Ben Everett?" the girl asked, with a dazzling smile.

Ben stopped in his tracks. Taking a step back, he said, "No, you must be mistaken." Abbi could feel the tension radiating off him.

"I'm sure you're him. I've watched all your movies and I think I would know," she said, twirling her fingers in her hair.

Ben glanced back at Abbi, his grip tightening on hers.

"Come on, let's get out of here." He tugged her hand.

Abbi could see the urgency on his face; she gave him a nod of understanding.

Turning back around, Ben saw the blonde was now blocking their path. *Great, just what we need now,* he thought. "Look, I'm not him. So, I'm not sure what you want with us at this point. Do you mind moving aside so we can pass?" he asked politely.

"I mind," the blonde responded. "… and who is she, your mother?" she asked, snidely.

That did it! Abbi's eyes flashed daggers. Time to gear up to take a slug at the bitch. Dropping Ben's hand, she rolled up her sleeves and took a step towards her target. She was stopped by two strong arms coming around her waist.

"Ben!" she hissed softly. "Put me down!" she yelled, kicking the air.

He did, after pivoting on his heel, placing her in the opposite direction. "Let me handle this," he said, dropping a quick kiss on her lips before turning around.

"What's your name?" he asked the blonde.

"Claire," she said with a triumphant smile.

"Claire… right. You see this lady you insulted…" he wrapped his arm around Abbi's waist, "… not that it's any of your business... is my girlfriend."

Claire snorted in derision. She was about to say something when Ben held up a hand. The anger in his eyes shutting her up. "Even if I was Ben Everett… which I'm not, what makes you think I would ever be interested in someone as shallow as you?" he inquired.

Claire looked ready to scream her head off, Abbi noted with a smirk.

Tossing her hair, the girl turned and stalked away without a parting word.

Looking at Abbi, Ben smiled. He moved his arm from

around her waist to her shoulders and leaned over, saying, "Come on Luv," as he planted a kiss on her brow.

Dear God, it will be so hard to tell him I can't do this, she thought as they paid for their purchase.

Getting to the outer doors of the mall, they were met with a downpour. *Perfect. It matches my mood*, Abbi thought, frowning at the sky.

"Wait here and I'll go get the car," Ben called, as he dashed to where they had parked.

Abbi waited for Ben to pull up. With a heavy sigh, she wondered how she could bring up that there was no way she could do what he asked of her. The two incidents hit home. Two pretty girls in one day, flirting with him. She'd forever live in fear, never being able to compete with all these women.

Ben ran to the car, laughing to himself as he went. He couldn't believe Abbi would hit that girl! He adored her when she was spitting mad. He had to stop her, though. That's all either of them would have needed… her getting arrested for assault. The way people took videos of everything, it would have been on the Internet faster than it took him to put the girl in her place. Unlocking the car, he jumped in, started the engine, and drove as close as possible to Abbi's side.

She was about to take a step towards the car when a man appeared from out of nowhere, bumping into her. Abbi glanced up startled, "Oops, sorry!" she said as he steadied her. *That's odd… Why would anyone be wearing a winter hat and gloves in this kind of weather?*

"No worries," he responded, holding on to her a little too long for her liking.

"Sure, well, have a good day," she said skirting around him to get into the car.

Ben leaned across her seat. He grabbed the handle and pushed it open for her; he noticed she was talking to someone. *Okay, bud, you can let go of her now,* annoyance flared in him. He

58

saw how uncomfortable she looked. He reached for his door handle, intending to intervene just as she backed away and went around the man to climb into the car.

"Wow!" Abbi jumped in, slamming the door she wiped her face off. "This rain is *crazy!*" She said trying to sop up the water from her hair with a tissue.

"Who was that?" Ben asked, reaching in the back.

"Who?" Abbi looked around. "Oh, you mean that guy? No idea, he came from out of nowhere and just about plowed into me."

"Right." He produced a towel from the back seat. "Here, use this."

She gave a disgusted look at him.

"It's clean, don't worry," he said, laughing, pulling away from the curb.

"Thanks," she mumbled, drying her hair. She sat there, staring out the window. The countryside replaced the city view. Debating on how to bring up being just friends, she realized he was pulling off to the side of the road. She turned, looking at him quizzically.

"Sorry, I need to dry off a bit, myself," he stated. She watched him remove his seat belt, followed by his jacket. Her eyes grew larger when she saw him reach for the hem of his shirt, as if in slow motion. She had no choice but to watch as he removed it. She had a choice, but her eyes just wouldn't let her. With each inch, it revealed his smooth muscled torso. A narrow line of hair traveled down from his navel, disappearing past his jeans. He had to have heard her throat as she tried to swallow. His skin looked as if it was made of satin. Goosebumps rose on his stomach. She resisted the urge to smooth them away with the heat of her hands. She fought with herself.

Her eyes trailed onward. Twisting her hands in the towel on her lap, preventing her from touching his abs and his wonderfully defined chest, his eyes... *wait, what?* He caught her staring. For the life of her, she couldn't look away. The heated look he tossed her way made her insides flop, tingle, and tighten. *Good grief, how am I ever going to stop this?* He reached over to take the towel off her lap, giving it a hard tug to free it from her grip.

Drying himself off, he said, "You never told me what upset you so."

"Huh?" she asked with uncertainty, for the life of her she had no clue what he just said.

"On the way up. You seemed terrified of me. I thought I must have done something to upset you like that." He grabbed a shirt from the back seat, pulling it on.

"Well?" he raised a brow waiting for her response.

She remembered now and didn't want to talk about it, but he had a right to know. Looking down at her hands, she took a deep breath. "Before I moved here, shortly after my book topped the bestsellers list, I would interact with my readers. I don't call them fans… I mean, I'm not famous by any means."

She glanced over at him. He sat there, one hand on the steering wheel, the other on the gearshift. He watched her intently, listening to every word. She blew out a breath.

"Um, I would talk to them on social media and answer mail when I could. At that point, I started writing another novel, so I didn't have a lot of time. There was this one guy that was overly chatty." She took another glance at him.

He was thoughtfully rubbing his chin, watching her, waiting. "So, kind of like what you're doing now?" he smiled. He could tell from her actions she didn't want to talk about it, but he didn't say that. He needed to know what happened.

With a slight smile followed by a wince, she said, "Yeah, I'm sorry. This is just really hard to talk about."
He encouraged her to take her time.

"Okay, so being busy I couldn't respond as quickly as he wanted me to. He started acting possessive, as strange as that sounds. He talked as if we were dating."

She touched his hand for emphasis. He took the

opportunity, turning his hand over, lacing his fingers with hers. She gripped tightly, her knuckles turning white.

"He started sending letters and packages to my house. When I ignored him, they became threatening." She stopped, tears spilling from her eyes.

"There was more to it, wasn't there, Abbi?" Ben spoke softly, leaned over and turned her face toward his, looking into her eyes. "Tell Me, Luv. What did he say?"

"He said, that if I didn't start talking to him again..." she paused, "that he'd take me away, use me... then bury me where no one would ever find me."

Sadness filled him with her words. He pulled her towards him as she collapsed against his chest, sobbing. "My God, Abbi. I'm so sorry you went through that." With tears forming in his own eyes he said, "Shh, It's okay, I'm here now." He soothingly stroked her hair then pulled back only long enough to look down, kissing her tears away. "I won't let anyone hurt you ever again."

Abbi had never felt safer than she did at that very moment. His soothing touch made her want more. Her lips sought his, softly at first, then with more urgency. He laid his hand against her jaw. Wrapping his fingers around the back of her neck he broke off the kiss, searching her fevered eyes.

"Are you sure?" His eyes burned with desire.

At her quick nod, he brought her closer, his lips brushing softly against hers. At her soft moan, he deepened the kiss. Their tongues seeking, tasting each other. They danced softly against one another, a ritual between man and women since the beginning of time. He bit her lip softly. Her soft whimper bringing him back to reality, to where they were at this very moment. He tore away from the softness of her mouth, resting his forehead against hers.

On a breathy sigh, she called to him, causing a smile to form on his lips. "Ben?"

"Yeah?" he answered.

"Take me home... now, please. I need a change of

underwear and a shower, and oddly, I feel like smoking a cigarette."

He howled with laughter. She felt spent, as if they had just taken a tumble in the sack. Abbi started giggling. She had never felt like that from a kiss. She could swear she just about had an orgasm, either that, or her window was down, and her seat got soaked from the rain. She needed to think about that for a bit, she softly smiled. For a few moments in time, they had been one; she thought crazily… not by body, but by mouth. She'd hold off for now on telling him this wouldn't work. For now, she was just going to enjoy the feelings that this man had awakened in her… feelings she hadn't experienced before

CHAPTER 9

Abbi was sitting there with a soft, satisfied smile on her lips. Her mind drifted to the preparations of the upcoming holiday, May Two-Four. In a few weeks, her kids would come up for the long weekend. Her brow furrowed. *Should I invite Ben?* She glanced at their clasped hands. How would her kids react to him? She knew Luke would be fine, but Ava and Lane... Well, that would be another story entirely. She knew they would disapprove and would tell her... and Ben. She could picture the encounter in her mind, and it wouldn't be pretty.

They were just coming out of the bend that would take them back to their side of the lake. She felt him lift their hands, softly kissing the back of hers. She glanced towards him to see him looking at her. Smiling at him, she turned her attention back to the road. A flash of black darted across the road in front of them towards the lake.

"Ben, look out!" she yelled, clenching his hand while bracing her other one on the dash.

He slammed on the brakes and came to a rocking stop. "What the hell was that?" he asked, searching the road.

She pushed her door open. "I think it was a dog," she tossed over her shoulder as she got out. Ben soon followed suit, joining her at the edge of trees that lined the road. He started whistling.

"Shh! Be quiet. It could have been a bear," she whispered, looking around with concern.

"A bear?" His brows shot up. "Huh," he said, thinking maybe his mum was right.

She looked at him. "Well, it is uncommon, but not unheard of. Come on, let's get going," she urged, walking back to the car. "Judging by its size it would be a cub. That would mean Momma isn't too far behind," she said, climbing in and slamming the door shut.

"*That's* the size of a cub?" he asked incredulously, as he got back in. At her nod, he blew out a breath. "I'd hate to see its mother." She laughed as he drove towards home.

Pulling into her laneway Ben asked, "Do you have any plans for the rest of the day?"

"Nope," she responded. "You know, the usual feeding of the brood." She motioned to the window where they all stood, looking.

Stopping the car, he threw the gearshift into park. He glanced at the window, a smile forming on his lips. "Right… right…. I don't think they would let you forget," he laughed. "After that, would you like to come over and give me a hand with the curtains?" His head down, he lifted his eyes to hers.

She couldn't resist him when he gave her that look.

"I can throw something on the grill, make a salad of sorts. It's the least I can do, seeing how you broke your plans today for me."

"Sounds good to me," she responded, getting out of the car. "Just let me feed these guys and I'll be over. An hour sound good to you?" she asked.

"Sounds perfect," he replied. *It will give me just enough time to clean up a bit.*

Shutting the door, she gave him a shy wave as she headed for the house.

Returning the wave, he backed up thinking about the mess that needed cleaning before she came over.

"Hey, guys!" Abbi called to them. Each one clamoring for her attention. Even Bird was excited to see her, landing on the dead tree that acted as a perch by the door.

"Come," she said to the dogs as they followed her to the back door to relieve themselves. The sun made its appearance once again, she noticed. Leaving the doors open wide, she returned to the kitchen to ready their food. Setting the dishes on the floor, the cats ambled over to eat.

"Bird, here's yours, sweetie," she said as she dumped his feed in the bowl on the dead tree. She went to her room to change into some sweats and a t-shirt. She grabbed a hoodie, just in case it cooled off too much, tying it around her waist. Returning to the kitchen, she saw both dogs finishing up their food. She went to the living room and closed and locked the French doors. After today's admission to Ben of what happened in the past, she felt uneasy about returning to an empty house after dark. She flicked the light switch that would flood the yard for her return.

"Lucy… Brutus, you guys want to go for a walk?" she asked them. They yipped and cried in response. Smiling, she said, "Good, let's go see Ben, shall we?" She had to laugh as Lucy whined, and Brutus bounded to the door, impatiently pawing at it, pausing only long enough to look at her as if to say, "come on, lady". She bent over to pick up Lucy, giving her a soft kiss on the head. "Let's go see your boyfriend." Grabbing her cell, she walked over to set the alarm. She locked the door, closing it with a soft thud.

Ben took the curtains out of the bag. From the back seat, he took his wet clothes and towel and stuffed them into it. He cast a critical eye on the rest of his items laying there. Hell, it looked like he was living out of his car. He really should get them into the house, too, he thought. Funny how Abbi never even commented on how his back seat looked like a dresser drawer. Any other woman would have criticized him for it. He would collect them up tomorrow, he decided as he climbed out of the car. Right now, he was pressed for time. Taking the steps two at a time, he reached with a jangle of his keys to unlock the door. He noticed something bunched up on the porch chair. That's odd, he thought, picking it up he held it, turning it around in his hands. *A jacket... Uh, that's not mine*, he thought, frowning, looking around for a car he knew wasn't there. He heard some footsteps coming from the side of the house. *Great... just great! The paparazzi found me!* Dropping the bag and curtains, he took angry strides towards the intruder. "Hey!" He called out, "Get the hell off my... whoa!" Rounding the corner, he almost collided with a tall, dark-haired man.

"Hey! Benny boy. How's it hanging?"

Immediate relief washed over Ben. Only two people dared called him that, his father and Mark. Grinning widely, "Mark my man," Ben gave him a hug. "It's great to see you." Turning around, Ben motioned for him to follow.

"Place looks good!" Mark commented as they headed to the door. "I had some time off, thought I would come and see how you're settling in," he said, picking up his jacket while he waited for Ben to unlock the door.

Shrugging, Ben said, "It's been good. I should have taken your advice and hired a cleaning crew," he laughed. "But it's all good now," he said pushing the door open. "Come on in. Make yourself at home. Where's your car?" Ben asked as he went to dump the wet bag into the washer. Adding some soap, he set the controls and walked back into the kitchen. He really needed to clean up a bit before Abbi arrived. He started stuffing dishes haphazardly into the dishwasher.

"Up the road a bit. I'm staying in the cabins there for a few days. Turned out nice after all the rains so decided to walk here," Mark said pulling a stool out from the center island and sat.

"Nice. Hey, do you want a beer?" Ben asked, reaching into the fridge not waiting for an answer from him.

Mark gave him a serious questioning look. "Uh, buddy, you

don't have to clean up on my account," he chuckled, motioning to the dishwasher.

Ben produced two frosty cold ones. Passing one to Mark over the island, he popped the cap on his. He took a long swallow before answering. "I'm not. Abbi will be here any minute," he answered, wiping his mouth with the back of his hand.

"Abbiii," Mark drawled out her name. "I like the sound of that," he said.

Ben turned away to wipe the sink down, his brow furrowed in thought. Mark was known as a ladies' man. He wasn't the type for a long-lasting relationship. At all.

"So, what does this Abbi look like?" Mark asked, fiddling with his beer cap.

Grabbing his beer, Ben tossed the rag into the sink and leaned back against the counter. "Um. She's nice." His eyes softened at the thought of her, a slight smile on his face. "Funny as hell, sweet, beautiful... you know what I mean?" He asked not really wanting an answer. Mark could see the reaction on Ben's face as he talked about her.

"You got it bad, don't you bud?" he grinned at him.

Ben wiped his mouth. "Yeah, is it that obvious?" he asked.

At Mark's nod, Ben felt the need to explain. "Stupid thing is, I've only known her for a couple of weeks. And been in her company three times. I can't seem to control myself around her... even kissed her already for God's sake! That's not like me... that's something you would do."

"Taking lessons, are you?"

Mark had to laugh at Ben's flustered state. Ben was never the guy to approach a woman at all. And to kiss one so soon... holy crap! It was funny as hell to see his friend shaken so much over one.

"Just do me a favor, don't come on to her, alright?"

"I don't know man, you know I can't help myself," Mark laughed.

Raising his brows, Ben said quietly, "I'm serious." He gestured with his hands to emphasize his point. "Abbi is different. I've never been this attracted to anyone so quickly. Truth be told, she scares the hell out of me."

"Why would she?" Mark questioned, all joking aside.

Letting out a sigh he said, "She's wary.... very wary." Pausing, he wondered if he should go on. He wasn't sure how his friend would react. Not that it mattered to him, he was being truthful with Abbi when he told her age meant nothing to him. "She's older than me."

Mark shrugged. "Okay... so what's the big deal?"

"By twelve years," Ben supplied, watching his reaction.

"Ha! Twelve years?" Mark waved his hand. "That's nothing! When I was twenty-five, I dated a woman who was fifty, age means nothing."

"*That's* what I said," Ben pointed to his chest. "But to her It's just wrong. She finally agreed to think about it though, so that's a plus."

"Look, man, if we men can date a nineteen-year-old when we are in our sixties, then so can women," Mark told him. "To hell with what's proper," he laughed. "Wait, she isn't a gold digger, is she? It's really easy to tell."

Ben was chuckling, shaking his head. "No man..." Mark held up his hand when Ben was about to speak.

"No... no, let me explain. Does she wear sexy clothes and flounce around when you're together, or does she come on to you, like at all, even subtlety?" he questioned.

Ben just stood there laughing.

"What's wrong with you, man? I'm serious," Mark hissed.

"Right, I know you are, and no, she is none of those things," Ben denied. "She actually avoided me at first," he smiled, remembering.

"You need to be sure Ben. Hell, she could take every penny you have ever made, be reasonable." Mark countered.

A knock on the door had them both looking up.

"Is that her?" Mark whispered, turning to look at Ben.

"Yeah, that will be her," Ben nodded, pushing away from the counter to go answer the door.

He thought he'd better set the record straight with Mark before letting her in. Stopping in his tracks to do just that, Mark bumped into him. Looking at him, Ben asked incredulously, "What are *you doing?!*" His voice raised with each word.

"I want to see!!" Mark exclaimed excitedly.

"Of course, you do," Ben rolled his eyes, "... from over there." He pointed to the chair Mark had just vacated from at the island. "And, before I let her in," he said to Mark's retreating back, "I'll answer your question. There is nothing wrong with me and she's not a gold digger. As a matter of fact, she likely has more money than I do, possibly the both of us," Ben stated, turning towards the door.

"What? Wait! How can she?" Mark pleaded, coming to a half stand.

Turning back, Ben replied, "She's an author, none other than Abbi Stevens," Ben smiled.

"Come again?" Mark blinked his eyes blankly.

Ben stood there with one hand on his waist and the other wiping down his face. "She wrote the book we are filming." He tilted his head and raised his brows. "You know... The Jasper Killings."

"Oh..." Mark trailed off sitting down in thought.

"Yeah, just what I thought you'd say," Ben laughed with a satisfied nod.

CHAPTER 10

Abbi stood on the porch looking at her watch for the tenth time. Maybe he fell asleep, she thought, or he ran to the store? *Why wouldn't he take his car?* she wondered, knowing she would be there soon. She glanced down. Both dogs were sitting right in front of the door. Their heads tilted from side to side every so often as if they heard something coming from inside. Maybe he was in the shower. Raising her hand to knock once more, the door abruptly opened.

"Oh, my goodness!" she jumped, laughing. "I just about knocked on your face."

Leaning one hand on the door frame, Ben smiled, gazing into her eyes. "Hi again, to you too." His eyes drank in the sight of her. He placed an arm around her waist, pulling her close. Leaning towards her, he placed a soft kiss on her mouth. "I missed you," he murmured against her lips, dipping for one more.

"Me too. Missed you, that is," she stammered.

A cough came from inside the house. At her questioning look, Ben sighed. "I have a guest."

"Oh?" she wondered.

The dogs decided it was their turn for Ben to pay them some much-needed attention. Brutus jumped up to get a hug.

Abbi cried in alarm, tugging on his collar, "Brutus! Get down!" She was no match for the beast.

70

"It's all good," he said, smiling, giving the big brute some love. He glanced down to see Lucy pawing the air for his attention as well. He scooped her up and was promptly awarded with kisses.

"I'm sorry for bringing them, I just hated to leave them behind again after such a long day," She explained.

Setting Lucy down, he replied, "It's fine, Abbi. I wouldn't expect you to," he told her then gave her another quick kiss.

The door swung open wider, revealing an attractive, tall man with jet black hair. He promptly stuck his hand out, giving her a charming smile. "Nice to meet you, Abbi. I've heard so much about you. The name's Mark Donovan. Ben and I are coworkers."

Smiling, she shook his hand. "Mark... nice to meet you." She glanced at Ben with a surprised look.

"Mark thought I was cleaning up for him," Ben explained as he stepped aside for her and the dogs to enter.

By Mark's standards she was average, pretty in her own way he supposed, but not someone he could see himself falling for. For starters, she was curvy, not the customary, supermodel thin. She had a pretty face, nice eyes, and lips, he noted. She could use a little makeup, he thought. Not the sort of woman that usually clamored around for attention. Maybe that was what attracted Ben to her?

"Yes, but he didn't mention how beautiful you are." Mark eyeballed her up and down as she passed by him. Ben shot him an incredulous look. Looking at Ben, he put his hand up to block his mouth from Abbi's view, just in case she turned around. Silently, he mouthed, she's hot, as he pointed towards her back. Ben gave him a warning look. Mark's response was a thumbs up followed by a huge grin. Shaking his head in disbelief, Ben walked over to the fridge, taking out a package of steaks. He figured the sooner he got the food cooked the sooner Mark would leave. He hoped. Ripping the package open, he placed them on a plate and added some seasonings.

"So, Abbi, Ben here told me you're a writer?" Mark asked.

"Well, I've written a book," she nodded with a smile. "I wouldn't really call myself a writer," she added, taking a stool at the island.

"Beautiful and modest," Mark said, tipping his beer bottle in salute to Ben.

"Um, currently working on another," she added, not knowing how to react to that.

Ben noticed the immediate blush come to Abbi's cheeks. Protectiveness came over him. Taking a deep exasperated breath, he knew this is going to be a hell of a night.

Not wanting to embarrass her further he said, "Ah, Abbi. Would you like a glass of wine?" His gaze softened when he looked at her.

Nodding, she replied in a quiet voice, "Please, that would be nice."

He turned away to get a glass out of the cupboard.

Clearing her throat, she said, "Ben, I can get it." She got up and went around to him. She whispered, "Please, let me do this." He looked at her, concern filling his eyes. She nodded and said, "Go," giving him a gentle push, but not before he gave her hand a reassuring squeeze. Abbi walked over to the cupboard Ben had been reaching for.

The guys were in deep conversation, thank God. She didn't want to answer questions from Mark or make small talk at this point. She had nothing against the guy. She wasn't impressed by how he tried to... flirt? *Was that it?* she snickered. Whatever it was, it wasn't happening. She grabbed the closest glass. She didn't bother looking for a wine glass. All she cared about was that it held liquid. Searching under the counter for a bottle of wine, she came up dry. She looked in the cupboards and found a bottle. Excitement bubbled up inside her at finding it... until she read the label. *Oh... Cooking Sherry, hmm, it might just do.* Unscrewing the top, she took a whiff, wrinkling her nose, she jerked back. She risked a glance at the guys. Shrugging, she tilted the bottle back, taking a swig from the bottle. *Oh God, this is disgusting!* Rushing to the sink she spit it out.

Ben was watching her with an amused grin. "It's in the fridge, Abbi," he supplied.

"Thanks," she said gasping, wiping her mouth with the back of her hand. She replaced the Sherry in the cupboard and headed towards the fridge. Opening the door, she grabbed the bottle... red, her favorite, and chilled, too! Just the way she liked it. *Crap,* it wasn't a twist-off. She pulled out a drawer in search of a corkscrew.

Ben said, "... in the utensil holder."

"Right!" she said with a happy smile. She hated corks, all the bits falling into the wine after she struggled with the damned things. On that thought, she decided she hated corkscrews, too. She stood there struggling for a bit until she felt two arms come around her. She froze. A moment of panic set in until she realized, she knew those arms, causing her to relax immediately.

"Need a hand?" his voice murmured next to her ear.

Sweet heavens, he does crazy things to me with that voice! She stumbled back against the wall of his chest. His lips brushed the side of her neck as he breathed in her scent.

"Did I mention how sexy you look in sweats?" he asked huskily. His hips moved forward against her backside. *Oh, my word!* She let out a soft, whimpering moan.

She heard a door bang in the other room. *Mark!* Horrified, she looked up at Ben.

"Relax, sweet one," he said, dropping a kiss on her nose. "He's outside starting the BBQ." Dropping his arms, he took the corkscrew and bottle, skillfully opening it. He poured some into her waiting glass.

"Here," handing it to her. "I'll take this out to him." Ben

grabbed the plate of steaks. His brow furrowed. *I shouldn't have done that. This woman is driving me to do crazy things. Where the hell is your self-control man!* Heading towards the door to join Mark on the porch, he felt the need to reassure her. Stopping he said, "Abbi." He turned to look at her, waiting for her to look at him. "Just so you know…" he paused… "what we just shared will always be just for our eyes only. That is when you're ready, and the time is right." He could feel the desire rising again at the mere thought of it. "That is… if you want me," he hurried on, "I would never say or do anything in front of anyone that would make you uncomfortable or cause you to lose your trust in me, okay?" He needed to hear her response. "I'm sorry I should have told you straight away that Mark was outside," he replied, upset with himself.

He watched her gulp down her wine as she came towards him. Setting the empty glass on the counter, Abbi took the plate from him. She walked to the door calling out, "Mark, Ben just had to go to the washroom. He'll be right out." Handing the steaks over, she closed the door with a soft click. She walked straight over to Ben.

Great, she's going to rip me a new one. He watched as she stopped before him. Resting one hand on his chest, the other reaching up to touch the side of his face, she gazed deeply into his eyes. Tears were forming at the corners of her own.

"That's the nicest thing anyone has ever said to me." Reaching around to caress his neck, she felt goosebumps rising on his skin. With renewed confidence, she closed her eyes and placed a soft kiss on his lips. She felt his strong arms reach around her. *God, I love those arms,* she thought as he gathered her closer. She opened her mouth, allowing him to deepen the kiss with his searching tongue. This time when he brought his hips forward, she met him with a boldness she hadn't known she possessed. He moaned in restrained pleasure, his hands spanning her bottom, hiking her closer to him. She could feel his arousal, rock hard against her. Even though Abbi was aroused, probably more so than him, she was in control this time. She felt like a wanton wench and for once, she didn't care.

"Hey, Ben. Uh, we've got a bit of a fire going on here," Mark called from outside, an urgency raising in his voice.

They broke away from each other as if both were burned by an invisible flame. It took a moment to process what Mark had just yelled. Ben saw it first, the orange glow from the fire. Moving quickly, he threw a door open near the stove, grabbed a fire extinguisher, and ran outside with Abbi on his heels. The area around the BBQ was licking with flames. He pulled the pin, directed it at the flames, and pulled the trigger. Finally, the fire died down enough that it allowed him to slam the lid shut.

They stood, surveying the damage. The floor and railings would need to be painted or replaced in that area. Luckily, it had only scorched the ceiling of the porch that was all. Thank God it hadn't spread to the house.

"Sorry man. I was playing fetch with the dogs and by the time I noticed, it was shooting flames," Mark said apologetically.

"It's all good! I'm just happy it didn't spread further."

"So, who's up for pizza and wings?" Abbi inquired, clapping her hands together.

Mark held up his hand. "Me, I'm starving, but I'm buying, it's the least I can do."

She looked at Ben. "How about you, Ben? Are you hungry?" she asked, taking out her cell to call in the order.

"I'm famished," he winked, smiling at her.

Catching the innuendo, Abbi blushed. She could feel it, damn it. *Control yourself*, she yelled silently in her mind. Clearing her throat, she said, "All righty! I'll order it right now. Shouldn't take too long. I'll have it delivered."

Forty minutes later, they were all sitting out on the back patio, around the glass table, in comfortable oversized chairs. They had just finished eating and were drinking some beer as the sun made its way to set on another day. The loons called out over the still lake as Ben got up to light some torches around the patio. Abbi got up to collect the paper plates and takeout boxes to toss them in the recycling bin.

"Does anybody want anything else?" she asked, looking up from her task.

"I'm good," Mark said.

"No, thanks, Abbi. You don't need to clean this up," Ben said as he swept his hand at the mess.

"It's fine. I don't mind." she smiled in response heading towards the house.

Mark looked at Ben. "Tell me. Why did I sell this place to you again?" he asked, snickering.

"Good question," Ben responded, "I'm glad you did. It's honestly the best decision I have ever made in my life," he stated, watching Abbi through the kitchen window. She was standing at the sink, talking to herself. He smiled at the sight of her. She did that often when she thought no one was looking.

Mark glanced to where Ben was staring. "Yeah, I'll say. How long has she lived here?"

"Four years."

"To think, I could have been with her all this time. Good thing you got to her before me," Mark said, laughing, seeing now what Ben saw in her.

Ben gave him a deadpanned look and raised a brow to question. "What makes you think she'd be interested in you?"

"Come on," Mark said, holding his hands wide. "Who wouldn't want a piece of this." He gestured with his hands as if he were showcasing a prize on a game show.

Ben just about busted his gut. Laughing, he nodded towards the house. "She wouldn't, I can guarantee it," he smiled.

"Given the chance, I bet she would... if you weren't together," Mark said seriously. "Wanna bet on it?" he asked with a dare. He reached for his wallet. "I'll even put money on it," he said, laying a hundred on the table.

After some thought Ben replied, "Right! All right." Hesitantly, he reached for his wallet. Matching Mark's bet he said, "But," pointing a finger at him, "there are some conditions." Ben leaned forward, crossing his arms in front of him on the table.

Mark asked, "You will actually let me make my moves on your girl, right?" He raised his brows in question.

Ben gave him a stony look. "First off, she isn't my girl... at least not yet." *Soon, I hope...* "No... You can't make your moves. And yes, that's the first condition and don't forget it!"

"Come on, man!" Mark held out a hand. "How is *that* a condition? You're not even in a relationship with her." He threw his hands up.

Ignoring his outburst, Ben continued. "And second, you lay a finger on her... at all, I'll deck you," he threatened.

At the thought of the prospect of winning, Mark let out a triumphant, "Hell, yeah!" as he fist-pumped the air.

What the hell did I just agree to? What if she falls for Mark? He didn't want to pressure Abbi into being with him. His gut, his mind, and more importantly, his heart was telling him everything was right with her. He remembered the spark he felt the first time he met her, shaking her hand. The first night, lying on her kitchen floor, and that first kiss they had shared, had him wanting more. Earlier... in his car, and that moment hours ago in his kitchen had touched his soul. Whenever he was with her, he felt that spark. If those moments were the last, he ever

shared with her, he would forever cherish them... forever long for them, but he would let her go if it made her happy. Raising his head, he saw Abbi close the patio door. Her eyes were seeking him out, a smile for him on her lips.

"Um... one more thing," Ben breathed. "You have twenty-four hours."

"What?" Mark cried out in protest, spitting out the word.

"One… day," Ben clarified. Meeting Abbi's gaze, through the window, he sent a sad smile her way. Maybe it would help her decide what she wanted. He could only hope it was him.

CHAPTER 11

Abbi was trying to stay busy in the house. The dogs were laying under the table in the dining room. Glancing at her watch, she saw that only fifteen minutes had passed. Looking out the window above the sink, she saw the guys in deep discussion. *Is that… sadness on Ben's face?* she wondered. Walking to the patio doors, she gave a sharp whistle, calling the dogs. It was time they went out and she needed to wipe that sadness from his face; to hell with what Mark thought. Determined, she closed the door. Looking at Ben, a soft smile formed on her lips. Mark spoke first, "Abbi, sweetheart! So glad you decided to join us," as he dragged her chair towards him. "Why don't you sit your lovely self, right here…" he patted the seat.

He gave her what she could only describe as a leering smile. A creepy feeling tingled across her scalp. *What the hell did I miss?* Concerned, she looked at Ben. He turned away, leaned back in his chair and let out a sigh.

Arching a brow at Mark she said, "No. I'm good, thanks. I think I'll just head back home now." She saw Ben tense at her response. She wanted nothing more than to bend down and make him look her in the eyes.

"No! … I mean, don't do that, don't leave yet," Mark pleaded.

"Oh-kay then." She grabbed the back of the chair Mark had pulled over to his side. "I'll just move over here," she said, tugging on it to drag it away. She met resistance. Looking down, she saw him staring up at her, a smile on his face holding onto it. Determined, she tugged on it harder to no avail. She took a quick glance in Ben's direction. He didn't say a word. As a matter of fact, he seemed uninterested in the ensuing tug of war. Giving a defeated huff, Abbi looked around for another chair. There were only three. *Well, I'll fix them both.*

"You can have that chair, Mark." she scooped up Lucy, setting her on it. She sent him a smile. "Lucy will keep you company."

She glided over to Ben; he glanced at her, deep in thought.

"Scoot your chair back."

Ben pushed back away from the table. He started to rise to give her his seat, but she put a staying hand on his shoulder. "No, you're good," she protested, shaking her head. "Do you mind if I sit?" she asked, innocently pointing to his lap.

Ben shot Mark a surprised look before locking eyes with Abbi. She saw the immediate change come over him. His eyes lit up at her request. His lips curved into a soft smile. Shimmying back, he patted his thighs. "Course not, Luv."

Guiding her onto his lap, he placed a hand on her hip, leaving it there. Abbi sat down with a satisfied sigh. She felt his warm hard body pressed up against her backside. He made her feel safe, wanted, and loved. Well, maybe not love, she thought. It was too soon to tell, really. He reached out taking her hand in his and began to trace soft circles on her palm with his thumb. Oh! She thought with delightful surprise when she felt him doing the same to her hip. She could really get used to this. As wonderful as it felt, she reached for the hand at her hip and brought it to cross over her stomach, holding it there with hers.

"So, Mark, how did you two meet?" she asked, genuinely interested. Leaning back against Ben's chest, she looked across at

Mark. Was he scowling? She wondered.

Mark gave her a quick smile. "Well, it was on a movie set, what… three years ago now, Ben?" he asked.

Ben leaned forward a bit, looking around Abbi. "Yeah, that's about right mate," giving him a victorious smile. He leaned back in his chair.

Mark just rolled his eyes. "Yeah, thought so… mate," he sarcastically returned.

"Nice! What movie was it?" she asked, wondering if she had ever seen it, as Ben shifted under her.

Great, I'm likely putting his legs to sleep. She moved her bum over towards his other leg, trying to ease some of her weight. *What the heck is that poking me in the butt?* She shifted, trying to push it out of the way. *Maybe it's his wallet? No, guys don't carry their wallets in the front pocket. Well, maybe some do, but no, Ben took it out of his back pocket. It must be his cellphone.* She was listening intently to Mark explain all about the movie when she heard a humming. She looked around for the culprit. Glancing down at the table, she saw that it was a cell phone. Ben's cell phone. *How can that be… unless he's hiding one…*

Freeing her hand from his, she leaned forward, lifting her bum. She slipped her hand between them. Patting around for the protruding object, she could feel Ben shaking with laughter… something Mark must have said had him laughing she supposed. She herself had long giving up listening to his chatter. Her fingers found what they were searching for. She squinted her eyes in concentrated thought. Touching it with just her fingertips, she ran them along the length. She was trying to identify in her mind what it was. It was long, almost twice the length of her hand from wrist to fingertip. No, about a hand and a half, she decided. And, felt like a… *That's not a cell phone!* Her mind screamed in horror. She snatched her hand away, banging it on the underside of the table.

"*Ouch!*" she yelled as her eyes bugged out of her head. *Good*

Lord! I was playing with his penis! She must have scared the hell out of Mark, for his brown eyes darkened, a flash of concern on his brow.

He braced his hands on the table yelling, *"Whoa!"* Leaning away he added, "Abbi are you all *right*? I thought your eyes were gonna pop out of your head for a minute there, it looked like you were *possessed*," he said, practically spitting out his words, as he leaned forward to emphasize them.

Ben let out a bark of laughter.

Thinking quick on the spot was never one of her strong suits. She darted her eyes everywhere, avoiding Mark's face.

"Sorry, I didn't mean to scare you," she said, "I, uh… a spider ran across my hand… I think… and I hit it on the table when I jerked it up. Yeah, that's what happened," she nodded, happy with her excuse.

Ben was in tears at this point, but managed to say, "That's your story and you're sticking to it, is that right Abbi?" He peeled out another bout of fresh laughter.

I'll get you back. She moved her hips ever so slightly, just enough to make him squirm. His laughter immediately stopped. She could feel the heat of his body as he moved closer. She briefly closed her eyes, masking the pleasure of his breath on her nape.

Try as he might, Ben lost all self-control when she started squirming in his lap. Thankfully, it was dark enough, and he was behind Abbi so Mark couldn't see the sweet torture she was putting him through. Leaning forward, he inhaled the intoxicating scent of her. Breathing harder, he buried his face in her hair at the back of her neck, placing his lips there, a desperate need to touch her. She was pure madness… He didn't know how much more he could take.

Mark turned his head and raised his brow. "Uh, hey, buddy. Ben, you all right?"

Coming back to reality, Ben took a deep breath, feigning a loud yawn. He stretched his arms, bringing them forward to encircle Abbi within them. He lightly kissed the side of her neck. "Yeah, just tired, you know?" he responded, glancing towards Mark.

Mark looked at both as if each had grown a set of horns. "You both are nuts," he said, throwing up his hands in defeat. "You're perfect for each other," he stated with a laugh.

Knowing it was time to go, Mark stood up. "Well, I best be going," he said.

Abbi got up as well, followed quickly by Ben. He grabbed a hold of her shoulders, using her to block Mark from seeing exactly what was wrong with him.

"That money there," Ben motioned with his head towards their bet on the table. "Take it, dinner is on me," he said.

"Nah, you keep it. Take your beautiful lady here out on a fancy date for me," he said. Smiling, he said, "Abbi, it was a pleasure meeting you." He took her hand, bowing his head; he planted a quick kiss on the back of it.

"Ben is one of the best guys I know. He will treat you right. But if you ever tire of him, look me up," he shot her a wink. With a salute to Ben, he turned on his heel, walking down the driveway.

Abbi stood there. She dared not look at Ben. She had done the one thing he had promised he wouldn't do, make her feel uncomfortable in front of someone. She had to say something, tell him she was sorry. Slowly she turned around. With eyes downcast, she took hold of his waist. Bending her head down, she leaned it on his chest, staring at the ground.

"Um, I wanted…" She felt him lift her chin. She had no choice but to look into his eyes. "Ben I…" The hungry urgency of his lips silenced her. His hand slid to caress her jawline as he held her to him, deepening the kiss. The growl emitting from his throat caused a liquid fire to shoot through her soul. He was like a drug, one that she was quickly becoming addicted to. Placing her hands on his arms, she pushed down as she tore her mouth away. Looking into his eyes clouded with desire had her almost caving. She held her hands together, preventing them from seeking him out. "Ben, I have to tell you how sorry I am for doing that with Mark being here," she whispered.

"Abbi," he said, "there is no need to apologize."

"Oh, but there is. Please... let me finish. I did the unthinkable, something just a couple of hours ago that you said you would never do to me, I'm sorry for that, I broke your trust."

Ben took a step towards her, reaching out. She knew he'd hug her, something she just couldn't handle now.

"No. Stay there." At his wounded look, she explained, "Every time we touch, I lose my mind. I'm not used to these feelings you stir in me. It's been a very long time, if ever, that I've felt this way."

Hearing those words come from her lips made him feel elated. There was hope. He knew then he had to take things slow; otherwise, she'd back off. She would close herself off and he'd lose her forever. "If I promise to keep myself under control, can I hug you?" he asked softly, raising his brows.

A slow smile formed on her lips. He opened his arms wide as she gave him a slight nod. Embracing her, he knew he had to tell her about the bet with Mark

"Now I have something to confess," he sighed.

Looking up, Abbi stared into his eyes, waiting.

"You know that money Mark left behind?" he asked. He tucked a curl away that had fallen over her eye. He loved looking into her eyes.

At her nod, he took a deep breath.

"He bet me he could get you... interested in him." He rushed on... "I told him there was no way that you would, but he insisted you would and so he bet me." He could feel her tense up.

"Why did you do that?" she asked sadly.

He saw the hurt in her eyes and hesitated for a second. "I did it because of how I feel for you, Abbi. I don't want it to seem like I'm pressuring you... I thought perhaps it would help you decide what you want."

Her arms went around him, giving a tight squeeze.

"Mark's a guy who will flirt... relationship or not, with anyone." He hugged her tighter. "So, I matched his bet with some conditions." He kissed her forehead. "I'm so sorry I did that Abbi. I felt like I had lost any chance of being with you."

Knowing why he looked so sad earlier, she laid her head on his shoulder and asked, "What were the conditions?"

Ben looked up, gazing in thought. "He asked me if I would let him put the moves on you. I said no, he couldn't, and that was a condition he better remember. He objected, of course, but I ignored him." He could feel her slight chuckle at that. "The second condition was that he wasn't to lay a finger on you at all, or I would deck him." He heard her sniffle as her arms tightened around him. "... and the third condition... he had twenty-four hours."

"Twenty-four hours?" she asked, looking at him in confusion.

Leaning back, he lifted her chin, searching her eyes. They were glistening with tears. "Yeah. It happened one moonlit night... the day we met," he breathed. He watched a single teardrop slip down her cheek. "I gave him the same time it took me to fall for you," he said, softly kissing her tears away. Still holding her, he leaned back, not wanting things to get out of hand again. He gathered her close, dropping an innocent kiss on her hair.

CHAPTER 12

"Oh, for Pete's sake!" Abbi pushed back from her keyboard. The insistent cock-a-doodle-do of her ring tone was getting to her. *I really ought to change that to something less distracting... like silent mode.*

"Hello?" she snapped.

"Hey, Mom! What's wrong with you?" It was one of her sons.

"Lane! Nothing, uh, why do you ask?" she questioned suspiciously. Had he found out about her and Ben?

"No reason, it's just you sounded a little perturbed."

"Oh, sorry. I've just been writing for days and my agent was after me to get it done. How many times did you call me?"

"Well, that makes sense. Just once. Why?"

"Someone called a few times, so I just wondered. I'll check when we are through. So, what's up?" she asked.

"Oh, okay. Anyway, I'm calling about our plans for the long weekend. Luke, Cassie, and Ava will ride with me. We should be up there Thursday."

She rubbed the back of her neck. "Cassie? Who is Cassie?" she asked, confused.

"She's Luke's new girlfriend. They've been dating for like a month... kind of a floozy... a gold digger, if you ask me. I told him that too, but you know how Luke is."

She frowned. "Now Lane, that isn't a nice thing to say." *Great, how's he going to react to Ben?*

He snickered. "It's true, Mom! He always gets with someone out of his league or after his money."

Lane had a point. Now she was worried. "Ah, well, you know, it's his life, he's an adult. He can decide that for himself."

"Where is this coming from? That doesn't sound like you at all," he stated.

"People change, Lane," she said with a soft sigh. "Wait, did you say this coming Thursday… or next?"

Impossible, it couldn't have gone by that fast. She grabbed the calendar off her desk and looked at the date on her laptop. Had she been so consumed with writing lately that she didn't even know what day it was? It was this Thursday! It meant she hadn't talked to Ben for… five days?

She thought back to that last night they had been together. He had walked her and the dog's home after they had held each other while talking. He had been true to his word and kept his feelings in check. They kissed goodnight on her front porch with neither one of them wanting it to end. She had gone in the house with the dogs. Little did he know… she stood watching him through a crack in the curtains from the front window. He sat on her porch step for a bit before leaving. After a few minutes, he stood, pausing on the top step, glancing back at the door. It took everything in her power to resist flinging it open and grab him, never letting go.

Lane interrupted her musings. "Mom! Helloo, are you there? Can you hear me?"

Shaking her head, she answered him. "Yes, I can hear you. Sorry, my mind drifted off," she heard herself say.

"Well, you might want to do something about that then," he laughed into the phone.

"Oh, I will." She knew exactly what she'd do about that. No more wasting time. "Um, by the way. I will have a friend come by this weekend if he wants to."

"A friend? Oh, you mean, Mack?" Lane asked.

"Well, Mack is always invited out here, but no… his name is Ben," she mumbled, clearing her throat. "He moved to the house on the point about a month ago."

He paused before answering, "Oh, what kind of friend?"

The kind that you fall for without a care in the world… one who is almost young enough to be your kid. That kind of friend, Lane!

She heard muffled talking on his end, thank God.

"Hey Mom, I have to run. My meeting is just about to start, so I'll see you on Thursday, okay?"

"Sure thing, honey. You have a safe trip up here. I'll see you on Thursday. Love you." She hit the end button before he changed his mind and talked more.

Looking at her notifications, she saw that she had three missed calls from an unknown caller. Maybe Ben put his number in her phone without her knowledge. She'd have to mention it to him. She should take a break from writing. She hadn't left the house since starting, only stepping away from the computer long enough to take care of the animals and her personal needs. Glancing out the window, she noticed a dark blue car parked along the road. *Probably checking out the lake,* she thought dismissively. Her gaze drifted toward Ben's house. She felt like it had been forever since they had seen each other and decided she'd go visit him. Did he ever get around to hanging up the curtains he bought? she wondered, heading to take a shower.

Ben was trying to figure out an excuse to see Abbi. He was giving her space, but it was driving him crazy. The last time he saw her was the night on her porch. Kissing as the moonlight streamed down. He felt as if they were not alone. No one was around as far as he could tell, but something felt off for sure. The dogs didn't seem bothered; neither of them made a fuss. But he felt something was out of place. He stayed there for a bit, long after she had gone in, trying to hear in the darkness to see what it could be. Whatever it was, it had moved on. He wanted nothing more than to take her back to his house for the night but knew she wouldn't have it. It had been five days of not seeing her, five days of fighting with himself. He needed to see how she was doing, even if she turned him away.

Going into the utility room, he snapped open a toolbox. Checking the contents, he closed the lid and carried it out to the dining room table. Grabbing his jacket, he slipped it on. Picking up the toolbox, he took an apple from the fridge, biting it and holding it in his teeth as he snatched his keys from the side table. Opening the door, he glanced down. He frowned, *what the hell is that?* It looked like… dried blood… Sitting the toolbox on the porch; he bent down to get a better look at it. It made a dripping pattern as it came up the steps, pooled at the door, then dripped back down the steps again… towards Abbi's.

Ben immediately felt the panic rise in his throat. Slamming the door shut, he tossed the apple and sailed down the steps, running to Abbi's. Bounding up the steps, he pounded on her door. Why couldn't that woman ever answer her bloody door?

"Aargh!" he yelled, shoving his hands through his hair in frustration. Cupping his hands around his eyes, he peered through the window. The dogs weren't even there. Calming down a bit at that discovery he saw her car in the laneway. *Okay, maybe they walked to the store.* He cast his eyes to the road, looking to see if she was walking down it. All he saw was a dark blue car pulled off to the shoulder. He stalked back to the door. *What's one more round of pounding going to hurt?* He beat at it, shouting her name.

Abbi was standing in the shower. She rolled her neck as steamy water rained over her tired tight muscles. She could slowly feel the tension ease. *Sitting at a desk for the better part of a week will do that to you…*

Lucy and Brutus were waiting for her to step out of the shower, their tongues at the ready to lap the water droplets on her legs. She turned off the tap and jumped as Brutus gave a sharp bark. "What's the matter, boy?" She asked.

Stepping out, she grabbed a towel off the rack and wrapped it around her head. Lucy trailed after her, licking her legs as she walked over to the door. She took her robe off the hook and stopped. She heard something. Standing still to get a better listen, she waited. *Hmm, I must be hearing things...* She slipped on her robe. There it was again. *Okay, that's someone pounding very hard...* By the sounds of it, it was on her front door. She pulled the bathroom door open. The dogs shoved past her, running to the front door, barking their heads off. She ran into her room. Tossing on a sweatshirt and jeans, she ran to answer the door before whoever it was broke it down.

Ben stopped pounding when he heard the dogs barking on the other side. *What? They're not supposed to be here. Something has to be wrong with her. Why else did it take them so long to come running? Did they not want to leave her side?*

"That's it. I'm breaking the door down." Backing up as far as the porch edge would allow it, he took a deep breath, steeling himself for the impact. He knew he'd have to put his shoulder into it, it was going to hurt like hell.

"Here goes nothing." Taking a deep breath, he took a run at it, turning to put his shoulder into it. For good measure, he let out a yell that would match the call of any war cry in history.

Who in the world is yelling? Abbi flung open the door. "Sweet baby Jesus!" she jumped back just in time from being plowed into by... Ben?

Ben just kept going on... and yelling. The dogs gave chase as he landed with an "Oomph," smashing his shoulder on the floor. *Well, at least it wasn't the door*, he thought lying in pain. He didn't move.

"What the...?" Abbi stammered, slamming the door shut. She rushed to him. "Oh my God, Ben! Are you all right?"

He pulled himself to a sitting position. Looking up at her. "Yeah. Where were you?" he asked, annoyance etched on his face as he held his arm.

"What do you mean, *where was I*? I was here, taking a shower." She pointed to the towel on her head.

"Oh," he said, feeling like a fool. "Right… sorry," he mumbled.

"You're hurt. Come on, get up." She reached around his waist, helping him to his feet. "Here, sit down." She pulled out a chair at the table for him. "Take your jacket and shirt off."

He raised his brows in surprise.

"I want to look at your shoulder, silly," she smiled.

"Oh, sure," he said, taking a seat. "Bloody hell, you have a hard floor." He winced while slipping his jacket off, struggling to lift his arm.

"Um... Abbi, can you help with my shirt? I can't seem to lift my arm."

She steeled herself; she remembered what he looked like without a shirt. Maybe he should just go to the clinic. That was silly. It's likely bruised, no need for a clinic visit. "Yep, I can do that," she answered, lifting the hem of his shirt.

God, how I've missed her, he thought, breathing in her scent. He closed his eyes, hiding the heat from her, he knew was there. Her fingers accidentally grazed his stomach. He gasped at her touch, a touch that caused a shiver to run through him.

"Sorry, I'm trying not to hurt you any more than you already are," she mumbled.

"It's okay, I don't mind. I don't think it's too bad," he muffled into his shirt as she slipped it over his head.

She gently pulled it down his injured arm, sucking in a breath at the sight of it. She lightly laid a hand on his skin. "Oh my God! How bad does it hurt?" She was shocked to see it was already turning an angry purple.

"Um, not too bad, I suppose," he replied, lying.

Rushing to the fridge she pulled out the freezer drawer,

searching for an ice pack. Coming up empty, she grabbed a bag of frozen peas. She took a clean towel out of the drawer and wrapped the bag in it. Snatching a bottle of water from the fridge and some ibuprofen from the window ledge, Abbi went back to him.

"Here, take these." She handed him the pills and opened the water bottle before passing it to him. She took the wrapped peas and gently placed them on his shoulder. "Do you think you can move it at all?" she asked.

He did a bit. "I think it will be fine, just need a few days of rest," he said, looking up at her. "I'm sure it will be as good as new, then."

"Were you planning on breaking the door down?" she asked with a laugh.

"Actually, yes I was," he nodded. "I came over to fix your step before someone breaks their neck on it. But when I came out of my house, there was a trail of blood leading up the steps and back down again towards here," he told her, watching for a reaction.

"You thought it was me?"

"I thought something might have been wrong, yes. Something might have happened to you." He paused. "I panicked. Now I feel like a fool."

She watched the expressions play over his features. It touched Abbi, not only from what he said but what his face showed.

"Oh, before I forget, take my phone. It's in my jacket pocket there. Please put your number in for me," he said, reaching up with his good hand to take the peas from her.

Taking his cell out of his pocket, she glanced at him in confusion.

"What is it?" he asked, noticing the look that crossed her lovely face.

Shrugging she said, "Oh, it's nothing. I just had three missed unknown calls earlier. I thought it might have been you."

Ben sat rubbing his chin lost in thought.

"As I said, it's nothing… happens all the time." She placed his cell on the table. "Now, let me take another look."

He removed the bag of peas, looking up at her, noticing her brow furrowed with concern. She laid a hand over his shoulder. It felt warm but not hot, but then again, he did just have ice on it. She leaned over, ever so lightly brushing her lips over his skin.

"Um, sorry. I wasn't thinking." She shook her head, standing up. She realized she couldn't keep doing this to him. The problem was she couldn't help herself. She knew what she wanted, and that was him; she just didn't want her kids finding out. That would be a little hard with them coming up in a few days. There was no way she could stay away from Ben, nor did she want to. They needed to talk and the sooner the better.

"I think the pills are kicking in," he said, flexing his hand.

Thinking what her life would be like without him in it brought a sting to her eyes. Turning to him, she asked quietly, "Can you stay for a bit? We need to talk."

He saw the sadness in her eyes. In all honesty, what he saw in them made him want to fly back to England this second. "Um… sure, Abbi. I can stay," he replied, disheartened.

CHAPTER 13

Ben sat waiting for her to come join him on the back porch. He sat in the same chair that he had that first night of meeting her. He was thinking it was cruel to have him come out there. Since the minute he had seen the look on her face, he knew she was going to tell him she never wanted to see him again. He was scared as hell. It amazed him at how quickly the thought of losing her was turning him into a nervous wreck. He honestly didn't know if he could handle it. When his ex and he had split, he had made a promise to himself to never get involved with another woman unless he was sure she wanted the same thing. With Abbi, it was different. He was determined to show indifference; he had to. If this is what she wanted, then he just had to accept it. He wouldn't resort to begging, despite wanting to. He tensed as he felt the breeze when she passed by, heading to the other chair.

"Here you go," she said, setting a cup down beside him on the table and taking a seat. "I made us some tea," she said glancing at him. She took a double take. There he was sitting, looking straight ahead… looking as if he was carved from stone.

His shoulder must kill him….

She reached out to touch his thigh. "Ben are you okay?" she asked worriedly, studying his face. His gaze dropped to where her hand rested on his leg.

Abbi watched him lick his lips as confusion flashed across his handsome face.

Turning towards her, his eyes darted to her face. He cleared his throat as he was about to tell her to just get it over with, but he lost the nerve to do so.

"Ben, if you're hurting that bad, we need to go, now," she said.

Her panic made her words rushed. All he heard was '*need to go now*'. With a jerk of his head, he said, "Right, I won't bother you ever again." He moved to stand up.

She put out a hand to hold him in place. "Wait. What are you talking about?" she inquired. Her concern exploded. "Did you hit your head when you fell?" She laid a cool hand on his forehead. "My God, Ben, you're clammy!"

He reached up to grab her wrist; her touch was scorching to him. "Abbi, I'm fine. I have to go." He dropped her arm, pushing himself up with his good hand to stand.

She was faster. She planted herself in front of him, blocking him from moving. "Like hell you do, mister. The only place you're going is to the clinic or my couch, you decide." She stood, tapping her foot impatiently.

He looked up at her, giving her a laugh of derision. "What do you *want* from me, Abbi? Tell me now, please!" His eyes pleaded with her. "Because I really would like to know." He tore his gaze away, refusing to look at her.

Startled, she wondered where this was coming from. What had happened from the time he left the kitchen until now? "What I want from you is to know what the hell is bothering you," she responded softly, kneeling in front of him.

He looked like someone had just punched him in the gut. "How can you even ask me that? You said we needed to talk." He finally looked at her. "The look on your face said it all. I know you want me to leave you alone, so please, step aside so I can do that."

Abbi was wracking her brain trying to figure out what she had been thinking when she had said that. She remembered now. Yes, they needed to talk, talk about this weekend coming up, and how stressed she was for her kids to meet him. *Why is he giving up so easily?* Did everything we shared mean so little to him? She had to know. She couldn't just let him walk away without ever knowing.

"Will you look me in the eyes, please?" Abbi pleaded.

When he didn't move a muscle, she reached up to caress his cheek. He closed his eyes in response. *Why did she have to do that? And why am I still sitting here enduring this torture?*

"Ben, what do you want?" he heard her asking.

He turned his face towards her hand on his cheek. His mouth finding the center of her palm, he kissed her softly one last time before he backed away. "Abbi, what I want doesn't matter."

Dropping her hand, she said firmly, "Yes, it does."

"You're really *something*, aren't you? What do you want to hear, Abbi… hmm? Do you want to hear how the mere sight of you drives me insane?" Frustrated beyond belief he shoved his hands through his hair, wincing at the pain it caused. "Or how the scent of you makes my heart feel like it's going to jump out of my chest?" To hell with it, he'd pour his soul out to her. "How about when you touch me? It feels like a thousand bolts of lightning coursing through my veins, or when you kiss me… it's soft as a feather at first, brushing against my lips, then crashing into a crescendo of waves, drowning me…" He threw a hand in her direction, "… and you… you're my only lifeline." He banged his hand on his thigh in frustration and paused, finally, staring into her eyes… eyes he saw swimming with tears.

Taking a calming breath, he continued, "You want to know what else drives me insane with wanting?" he asked, softly, not waiting for a response. "... the way you talk to yourself when you think no one is around... the way you make me laugh when you're not even trying." He cupped her face with his hands and whispered softly, "... the way your eyes change from soft to smoldering with one blink, or the way your tears rip my soul apart, as they are doing right now."

That did it. Her tears were overflowing in streams down her face now. She didn't care that she was on the verge of an ugly cry, damn it. She... Did... Not... Care. Knowing he thought she wanted nothing to do with him crushed her. Then, to hear her described through his eyes was more than she could handle. She couldn't respond, for the life of her.

"I never wanted to tell you this. I never wanted to make you feel pressured into being with me," he said.

Ben wanted to rub his hands down her arms, to touch her back, hugging her fiercely to take her pain away, but he dared not. He knew if he did, he could never let her go.

"What I'm trying to say, Abbi," he lifted her chin, looking deeply into her eyes. "What I want is you, no one else but you. If that's something you want right now, not tomorrow... not next week, but today..." He paused, sighing, "then please no more waiting. Tell me what you want, because I *can't* keep doing this. I can't keep living, not knowing from day to day what I am to you... what I mean to you." He fell silent, waiting for her to tell him to get out.

There it goes. The ugly crying was happening. She placed her hands on his knees, clawing her way up onto his lap. Straddling his legs, she wrapped her arms around his neck. She laid her head on his shoulder, sobbing her face off. She felt his good arm come around her, followed slowly by the other, making her cry even harder. This man is not going anywhere, she decided as her tears subsided. She kissed the side of his neck. Leaning back, she placed her hands on either side of his face and searched his eyes.

"I'm sorry, I wet your shirt," she hiccupped stroking his face.

"It's fine," he smiled softly.

"No, it's not." Her voice broke, her face was going to do it again!

She silently screamed as fresh tears threatened. She pulled his face towards hers. Running her fingers through his hair, softly touching his lips with her own. She held on for dear life as she deepened the kiss. He broke it off, searching her eyes, her face captivating him.

"You have never been more beautiful to me than you are at this very moment," he murmured, his eyes dropping to her lips, then back up to her eyes, where tears spilled once more. Kissing them softly away, he whispered, "Does this mean no more waiting, no more guessing?"

She sat back on his thighs, planting her feet on either side of his legs. "Ahh," she exhaled a long breath as she wiped her eyes on her sleeves. She stopped to look at him. "How's your shoulder?" she asked, needing to know.

"Abbi, it's fine, still sore but getting better." He lied again.

"Good, good. I don't know how to tell you this. The reason I said we needed to talk was that my kids are coming up this weekend, should be here Thursday." She paused, looking at his expression. She thought for sure she'd see regret there when he realized she wasn't telling him she wanted nothing to do with him. "And I wanted to see if you would come here to celebrate with us." She covered her mouth with her hand waiting for his response.

"I'll come. But just so you know," he said as he took her hand away and held it, "everything I said to you, it came from my soul. I regret nothing."

He brought her hand to his lips, kissing the back of it as he looked into her eyes. He said, "Will you answer me now, please?"

She cleared her throat. "Just so you know, everything you said, how you feel about me, it's like you were reading my thoughts. I would be crazy to let that go... let you go... without seeing how things might be."

Ben had waited for what seemed like an eternity to hear those words from her sweet lips. He laid his hand against the side of her neck, guiding her to him, he lightly brushed her mouth with his. Passion rose sharp and swift as he clung to her mouth, deepening the kiss.

Brutus came barreling out the door, startling them apart. He headed straight to the water's edge. He started growling, pacing back and forth. Abbi got up from Ben's lap and stood. Looking out over the water, all she could see was a boat about 100 feet from her shore. Ben now saw it, too.

"Do you know them?" he asked as he stood with a frown, remembering the night he felt something was off.

"It's hard to make out the person, but the boat is a rental from down the road, must be someone on vacation." She shrugged it off. "Are you hungry?" she asked, taking a step into the house. "Those pills must be wearing off by now."

"Ah, yeah, a bit of both," he replied absently, turning to follow her in.

He stopped, glancing back towards the water. The boat was still there. God only knew how long it had been there before the dog had spied it. That uneasy feeling from a few nights ago was back. He gave a sharp whistle, calling Brutus back to the house. Waiting for the beast to bound up the steps, he didn't take his eyes off the boat. He didn't see a glint off a zoom lens, so he felt confident it wasn't the paparazzi. Brutus sailed through the door. Ben followed, closing and locking it behind him. If it wasn't the paparazzi, then who was it?

CHAPTER 14

Abbi was standing at the counter chopping vegetables for the stir-fry she was making for dinner. She put the animals' dishes down and Brutus was already devouring his. She wondered what was taking Ben so long. She could have sworn he was right behind her when she came into the house. Just as she was going to call out, he came around the corner, talking on his cell. From the sounds of it, he was getting frustrated.

"Mum, no... I'm... No. I'm good." Pausing, he moved the phone away, rolled his eyes, and returned it to his ear.

Smirking, Abbi continued to listen to the one-sided conversation.

"Yeah, Mum. Yes, I'm eating!" With another pause, he exclaimed, "No! You stay there! Put Dad on, will you? Yes, I love you, too." ... "Dad! Thank God! Will you..." Moving the phone away from his mouth, he groaned in frustration listening to his dad. He inhaled deeply as if counting to ten.

Impatience etched on his face. At that moment, Abbi thought he was beautiful. Could a man be considered beautiful? She decided this man could. She heard a sizzling... the telltale sound of the pan beginning to scorch. She whipped around to the stove just in time, before dinner was ruined.

"I'm good, Dad, more than good. That's why I need you to keep Mum there just a bit longer, you know?" He paused, listening. "I know she misses me. I miss both of you. But… I've met someone, Dad. Someone…"

Abbi turned back around as she heard Ben's father yelling from clear across the room. A grin broke out on his face.

"Her name is Abbi, and she's gorgeous," he said smiling, sending her a smoking look. "Yeah… right, right… yes, exactly! Thank you, Dad, I promise to let you know as soon as I can. All right? Love you, too. Bye."

Ben disconnected the call and walked directly over to Abbi. He brought his arm around her. Leaning down, he kissed the side of her neck just below her ear. A thrilling shiver raced along her spine as goosebumps played over her skin.

Breathlessly she said, "Dinner is ready," as she looked over her shoulder to meet his lips.

He turned her towards him, never breaking contact with her mouth. Deepening the kiss, he brought her up tight against his arousal. There was no way of mistaking that! She moaned in response. For better leverage, she grabbed hold of his shoulders. She heard his gasp of pain. *Oh, my goodness, his shoulder…!* Backing away, she looked up at him, concerned. "Let's eat, shall we? I'll get you more pain pills."

Pushing him towards the table, she grabbed the bottle from the window ledge and stuffed it in her pocket. She took two plates down from the cupboard, utensils from the drawer, grabbed a potholder and stuck a ladle in the pan, and headed to the table.

"I'm sorry. I don't do fancy around here." She smiled as she threw the potholder down, setting the frying pan on it. She passed a plate and a fork to him. "Eat, help yourself."

"Oh, before I forget… here." She opened the pill bottle, shaking out two tablets she sat them on the table. Getting up, she went to get drinks.

"Abbi, sit. You don't have to wait on me hand and foot," he replied with a happy grin.

"Relax! I'm just grabbing us a drink," she told him. "Believe you me, enjoy it while you can," she laughed, returning with two glasses of iced tea. "Besides, you only have one good hand at the moment. I don't mind." She took her seat, her eyes grew large as she looked down at her plate, noticing he had filled it. There was no way in hell she could finish all of that. "Look who's talking," she said, pointing at it, smiling as she picked up her fork.

With the first bite, Ben groaned in pure delight. "My God, Abbi this is delicious," he said, smacking his lips.

"Thanks," she laughed, watching him eat with gusto. "What have you been eating exactly since you moved here?" she questioned.

"Oh, you know," he shrugged. "Apples, eggs, and crisps," he laughed.

She shook her head. "No wonder you like this so much," she said. "So how are your parents doing?" she looked to him.

Grabbing a napkin, Ben wiped his mouth. "Good. My mum has been trying to convince my dad to fly over since the day I left, apparently," he chuckled.

"Really? That's sweet. I have to give her credit for her restraint, honestly. If it was one of my kids that moved across the world, I would have left an hour after them."

"Huh... I never really thought of it from her perspective before," Ben stated. "She drives me crazy at times, honestly, but she's my mum. It's her right, I guess."

"Damn straight it is," she laughed, getting up to take her plate to the sink.

"Wait, what are you doing with that?" he asked looking at her plate, licking his lips.

She paused. "Do you want it?" she asked, raising her brow.

"Sure!" he said, taking it from her.

Sitting back down, she said, "So, when you're done eating, I want to take another look at your shoulder." She looked at him with concern.

"It's fine Abbi, really it is," he lied.

If he was being honest, it felt like he broke something. He just didn't want to alarm her.

She shook her head. "I don't care. I'm looking at it. If it's worse, we are going to the clinic... and then you can stay here tonight when we get back," she added, softly looking at him through her lashes.

He looked up at her, with the last bit of food on his fork and stopped midway to his mouth. His face lit up. "Really?" His brows rose as a smile broke on his lips.

"Yes," she nodded. "In the spare room."

His face fell, recovering quickly with a stern look. He nodded. "Oh... Yeah, right, I knew that," he shrugged. *One day she will change her mind... maybe*

She laughed at him as she took the dirty dishes to the sink. "One day, perhaps... possibly soon," she added shyly. Walking back to him, she laid her hand on his back. "Time to let me see what's going on with your shoulder."

"You just enjoy seeing me with my shirt off," he teased, lifting the hem of his shirt.

"Guilty," she chuckled. She enjoyed seeing him with his shirt off; she wasn't going to lie. She loved how his muscles rippled under his skin. Once he freed his good arm, she helped him lift it over his head and down the other to expose his shoulder area.

No, no, no, that can't be good...

His shoulder was swollen. She laid her hand gently on his skin, trying to feel around for something out of place. She felt something but wasn't entirely sure what. The bruising had spread from the shoulder down his arm and up towards his neck. She stepped back and saw that it was noticeably lower.

"Does your neck hurt?" she asked.

He rotated it. "Hmm, a bit, nothing out of the ordinary, though."

"Try to look down," she replied.

He did and said with surprise, "Huh... my chest is bruised."

Abbi jerked her head around to look at his chest, her eyes darting everywhere *but* at the bruising. "Oh my," she sighed breathlessly.

"God, I just said that out loud, didn't I." *Damn it, and that too!*

She swallowed hard as Ben looked into her eyes, asking, "What do you suppose it is?"

"Um… it's your chest." She pointed to the bruising that she just now saw, felt her face go beet red, her heart racing.

Laughing, Ben grabbed her hand, laying it over his heart. "You do the same thing to me," he told her, holding her hand there.

She could feel the beat of his heart racing faster with just the touch of her hand. Leaning down, she placed her free hand on his thigh and looked him in the eyes.

"As much as I would love to sit here all night, we need to get you to the clinic… NOW," she said, planting a quick kiss on his lips. She took his shirt and helped him put it back on. He moved to get up, walking to the door he waited for her to join him.

"I'm ready. Let's go," she said, grabbing her keys and purse.

Ben opened the door to let her pass by. "Hey, aren't you going to set the alarm?" he questioned in surprise when she didn't.

"Nah, it'll be fine, the clinic is like two minutes from Mack's," she responded lightly.

"Abbi set the alarm, please," he said with a pressing tone in his voice.

She searched his face. "Okay, if it means that much to you," she punched in the code.

"It does," he quietly stated. Something was going on; he

had been playing this game far too long to be blind from what was happening. Someone was snooping around. He just wasn't sure who it was yet.

"So, it looks like you have a dislocated shoulder," Doc Spence said as he breezed into the examining room. He pulled up the x-ray on the computer screen and turned it for Ben and Abbi to see.

"Hell, no wonder it hurts like a bugger," Ben said, looking at the x-ray.

"Yup. So, what we need to do now is pop it back into place and put a brace on it, which you will need to wear for a few weeks for the swelling and pain to subside."

Doc Spence moved to a cabinet. Grabbing a syringe, he removed some medication from a small vial. He wiped down Ben's shoulder with a cotton ball wet with alcohol.

"Now, this will sting a bit, but only for a moment." He poked the needle in Ben's shoulder, pushing the plunger down. "It should only take a few minutes for the freezing to kick in. Be right back," he said as he headed out the door.

Abbi was sitting on a chair while Ben sat on the exam table. She reached over to rub his thigh. "You should have told me how bad it was hurting," she mumbled.

"Meh," he said, shrugging his good shoulder. "It's not a big deal, and we needed to hash out more important things," he said, taking her hand in his.

Just then the doctor returned. "How's it feeling?" he asked, taking out a tool to test the freezing.

"Good, I can't feel much of anything now," Ben answered.

"Great! I'll get you to lie down flat on your back," Doc said, taking Ben's arm as he did so.

"Abbi, I'll get you to go on the other side of Ben here and grip that sheet that's under him. Hang on tight, now. We don't want him slipping off the table."

Abbi balked at helping, but she jumped up and went around to the other side, gripping the sheet with both hands. "Now what?" she asked, licking her suddenly dry lips.

"Now lean back, he's pretty solid," Doc said.

You don't know the half of it, Doc... Abbi thought, flushing.

"Now slowly, throw your weight against it," he told her, doing the same as he gently tugged on Ben's arm, slowly rotating it as he did.

Abbi's heart went out to Ben as she watched a sheen of sweat break out on his skin, a grimace of pain etched on his handsome face.

"Yup, that's it," Doc said, "just... a... bit... more."

Abbi heard a pop, followed by immediate relief on Ben's face.

"There you go!" Doc said, moving Ben's arm at different angles. "There is still a bit of freezing, but how does that feel?"

"Much better."

Doc made his way to the door. "Awesome, once the freezing comes out, it will hurt like a bitch, so I'll write up a script for some pain meds, only take them as needed after the first day," Doc said, giving him a pointed look. At Ben's nod, he smacked the side of the door frame, tossing out "Good, be right back," and left.

Ben sat up on the edge of the bed and patted the spot beside him for Abbi to sit down. He put an arm around her, bringing her close.

"Thanks, Luv." He planted a kiss on her forehead.

She looked up at him. "For what?"

"For making me come here. For holding onto the sheet, when I could see that you clearly didn't want to," he chuckled.

"I didn't want to cause you any more pain. Honestly, I wanted to yell at him to stop, but, thought better of it," she smiled.

Doc returned with a script and handed it to Abbi. She got up and moved out of the way, so he could put the brace on Ben.

"Okay, so, keep this on for the first twenty-four hours at least. You can take it off to shower but immediately put it back on and make sure you keep it on while you sleep. That script I gave Abbi you can fill it at the pharmacy next door. I checked and they have it in stock. Also, do you have someone at home with you?" He looked at Ben.

"Uh, no I don't, it's just me."

Doc turned to Abbi. "He can't be left alone... not while on those pills."

She nodded her understanding. "He will stay with me," she said, darting a glance at Ben.

Turning back to Ben, Doc said, "I gave you enough for five days. Come back if it doesn't start feeling better by then. And I repeat... only take them as prescribed, starting when you get home." Before stepping away, Doc added, "Oh, before I forget, can you sign this?"

Doc Spence handed him his prescription pad. At Ben's questioning look he said, "I'm a huge fan, seen all your movies," he chuckled.

Ben let out a bark of laughter at the doctor's admission. "Right, sure," he said, smiling as he took the proffered pen. He scribbled on the pad and handed it back.

"Thanks, Doc," he said, holding out his good hand to shake.

"You're welcome. Abbi, you got a minute?" Doc asked, jerking his head towards the waiting area.

"Oh, yup," she said, getting up to follow him.

Great, he's going to ask me what's going on...

Her and Doc Spence had known each other since she moved here. They had gone to Mack's a few times for a coffee, but that's as far it went.

"What's up?" she asked when she was out of Ben's earshot.

107

He took his glasses off. "Those pills I gave him… if he acts out of sorts at all, call me immediately. They are highly addictive."

"Can't you give him something else? What about an over-the-counter pain med?"

He shook his head. "Wouldn't even touch the pain he will be feeling in the next 48 hours. I called the pharmacy to see what they had in stock before I even mentioned it, knowing he'd need something. That's all they have."

"What if something was shipped in? Just give him a couple of days' worth. Would that be okay?" she asked, concerned, "I mean, he is an adult so I can't decide for him…" she trailed off.

"We will leave it as it is, for now. He's only to get one every 12 hours. I'll call in the morning to Springbank and see if I can get something brought in. If I can, I'll just put the order in and get it sent out to your house?" he asked.

Nodding she replied, "Yeah, that's fine."

"Another thing. What's going on between you two?" He looked at her with a smile, leaning against the secretary's desk. He folded his arms across his chest… waiting.

"Whatever do you mean, Doc?" she looked at him innocently.

"Come on, Abbi," he motioned with his hand, "a blind man could see the way you two look at each other."

Blushing to the tips of her roots, she cleared her throat. "Um, well… whatever you think is going on between us," she gave a quick nod as she continued, "… is going on."

Here it comes, he's going to tell me I'm robbing the damned cradle. She braced for the impact of those words.

"That's… awesome!" he said, his face breaking out into a huge grin. "Honestly, Abbi, I think that's great!"

He grabbed her in a bear hug, just as Ben stepped out of the exam room. Seeing Abbi in the arms of the doctor brought an immediate sense of jealousy to Ben. He never felt like that before. *Wow man, get a grip, they're friends…* He cleared his throat to make his arrival known.

"Hey, Ben." The doctor dropped his arms and took a step towards him, holding his arms out. "I have to congratulate the man that captured our Abbi's heart here... didn't think that would ever happen," he said with a chuckle, putting his arms around Ben to hug him, too. "Whoops watch that arm," he laughed, smacking Ben on the back.

Ben felt like a fool, jumping to the worst-case scenario for nothing. He'd been doing a lot of that lately. "Thanks. It wasn't easy." Glancing at Abbi, Ben said, "She gave me a run for my money, and I'd do it all over again, every day of my life if I had to," he spoke to her, forgetting that the doctor was still there.

Abbi held out her hand, wiggling her fingers. "Come on. Let's go home."

They waved their goodbyes to Doc as they walked out to her waiting car.

She was just about to pull away from the curb. "Damn, I forgot your meds." She threw the gearshift into park and reached to take her seat belt off when she felt his hand stopping her.

"Abbi just go home. I'll just take what you were giving me."

"But Doc said..."

Oh! She was cut off by his lips on hers. He moved so quickly he made her head spin. Good Lord, he made her melt.

He pulled away just far enough to mumble against her mouth. "Go home, now, please," quickly touching her mouth once more before sitting back in his seat.

She inhaled deeply to settle her racing heart. "Okay, I can do that," she nodded with determination.

Just before pulling onto the road she had a giddy thought. She didn't know if she should be happy or running in the other direction. Her mind was in overdrive. *I'm in for one hell of a ride, aren't I? Too late Abbi girl, you're head over heels for him...*

With a stupid grin on her face, she glanced over her shoulder before pulling onto the road.

Reaching over, a black-gloved hand lovingly stroked the blood-red roses that were lying on the seat next to them.

Hmm, interesting. She's hanging around Ben Everett a little too much... What does she see in HIM, when she can have ME? It's time I get noticed; I think. Yes, most definitely. He's sniffing around my Abbi just a little too much lately.

The hand crushed the flowers, destroying them, thorns and all. Blood dripped from the black glove. Oh well, what's a little more bloodshed. You would have thought the gift I left on lover boy's step would have backed him off. Some are harder to convince than others... cackling echoed along the empty road as they drove the familiar route to Abbi's house.

CHAPTER 15

It was almost dark as Abbi drove towards home. It was that time of night when headlights were not all that effective in lighting the way. Ben was awfully quiet. She took her eyes off the road for a second to look at him. Finding him asleep, she glanced back at the road. Quickly, she shot her arm out in front of him as she slammed on the brakes. Ben jerked awake looking around rapidly, not focusing on anything.

"What the bloody hell?" he asked, confused. He looked down at his chest where Abbi's hand laid. Grabbing hold of it, he wondered what she was doing. He looked over at her to find her staring out the windshield, shaking like a leaf. "Abbi, what the hell is wrong?" he asked, adrenaline racing through his veins. He looked to where she was staring. There, in the middle of the road, sat a medium-sized... bear?

"Is that the same bear we saw the other day?" he asked.

She looked at him as if he were insane.

"If that was the bear, how would I know? They all look the same. That's a dog, Ben, a shaggy, dirty black dog.... and I almost hit him," she said, taking her seat belt off. She reached into the back seat, producing a pair of gloves. She put them on as she opened her door and got out.

"Wait for me!" Ben said, struggling with his seat belt.

She paused, never taking her eyes off the mutt. Finally, he joined her in front of the car.

"Do you think he'll come to us?" Ben asked.

"I don't know. Let's find out," she quietly said, slowly walking towards the dog. "It's okay boy. We won't hurt you."

The dog responded by standing on all fours.

"I think he's going to dart, Abbi," Ben mumbled. "Let me try." He went down onto his knees, moving closer and closer to the dog. It took one step forward, slowly stretching out its nose to Ben's extended hand. Abbi saw the tail tucked between its legs; its coat was shimmering in the beam from the headlights.

"Be careful, it might lunge at you," she warned.

"It's okay. I'm not going to hurt you." The dog's tongue darted out to lick his hand. "That's right, we're here to help," he said, slowly getting to his feet. Just as slowly, he backed towards the car.

The dog took tentative steps towards him, only to stop and glance around. As it got closer, Abbi saw its fur was covered in blood.

"It's bleeding," she said with a cry.

Ben turned to look at her. "Are you certain?" At her nod, he told her, "I'll walk back to your place. Hopefully, it will follow."

"No, it's fine. If you can get him into the car, it will be faster." She got in behind the steering wheel.

"I don't want him bleeding all over your seats Abbi," he shook his head.

"Really it's fine. The seats will wash and by the looks of this guy, he needs some medical attention now."

"As long as you don't mind," he opened the back door. "Come on, my sweet," he softly called, patting the seat in hopes the dog would take the hint. He was relieved when it took one leap onto the seat, turning itself around to lie down. He slammed the door shut and got back in the front.

"Where will we find a vet this late at night?" he asked, glancing in the back where the dog let out a huge sigh.

"Well, this dog is in luck. Mack is a retired Veterinarian," she said. "Hopefully he's chipped so we can get him back to his owner."

"What will happen to him if there is no owner found?" he asked, deep in thought.

"It's hard to say, really. The closest shelter is in Springbank," she glanced at him. "Why... what are you thinking?"

"Oh, I'm just thinking if he has no home, I can take him in... I would need to figure out what I would do with him when I have to leave though."

"I could watch him over at my place. If he gets along with Brutus and Lucy, I don't mind," she offered.

"That would be great! Unless, of course, he has a home to go to."

She pulled beside Mack's store. "Let's find out," Abbi responded opening her door. "I'll just get Mack to come out for a minute." She turned and jogged into the store.

The dark blue car stopped on the side of the road. It was almost dark, so it would be easy to see Abbi flitting from room to room in her house.

Silly girl, she should close her curtains at night. But if she did that there would be no way for you to see her you fool! Hmm, the house was in darkness, that was odd. No car either... where did they go off to now? You should have been quicker at following them, the voice screamed. Panic struck with the thought of Abbi at Ben's house. I'll just drive by there... I'll say I'm lost if they ask... yes, that will work. I need to make a special delivery, but only when she's home, they stroked the broken roses. I'll just return later to place them lovingly on her doorstep...

Ben got out and opened the back door. "Come on, boy, let's get you looked at," he murmured to the sad eyes looking up at him.

Glancing up, he saw Abbi coming around the front of the car with Mack in tow.

"Hey, Mack," he said in greeting.

"Hi, Ben, how you doing?" Mack responded, leaning in the open door to get a look at the dog. "Where did you find him?"

"He was in the middle of the road, halfway back from the clinic," Abbi supplied.

"Okay. Can he walk?" Mack asked.

"Yeah, he can," Ben said as he called the dog out of the car.

"Let's get him into the back of the store."

Mack led the way, the others following him to the back of the building to a door. Taking out his keys, he unlocked it, pushing it open for them to enter.

"Abbi, will you watch the store for me for a bit, please? See that door there? Just go through it, and it will take you out by the washrooms," he said, jerking his head towards the door in question.

"Sure thing, Mack," she answered, making her way to it.

"Just leave it open in case we need a hand here. I'll yell for you if we do," Mack said as he got out his medical bag. "Okay. Let me see what we have. Can you give me a hand lifting him, Ben?" he asked.

"Yeah sure, I'll grab the rear if you can get the head," Ben said, showing him his arm.

"No problem! What did you do to it?" Mack asked, "Abbi fall on you or something?" he laughed.

"Nah, nothing like that," Ben chuckled. "It was my stupidity. I ran to her place after I noticed some blood on my porch, thinking she might have some trouble. She didn't answer at first, so I got the idea to bust her door down. I was going full tilt when she opened it," he laughed, as the event replayed in his mind. "I

114

crashed to her floor, and this happened." He moved his arm in reference. "Dislocated my shoulder. We were just heading back from the clinic when this guy appeared on the road," he said, petting the dog's head.

"Well, he's lucky you guys came along when you did," Mack said.

"How is he, Mack? Will he be okay?"

"Well, I'll give her some shots. Get her caught up on her vaccines, which, by the looks of it, she's sadly lacking," Mack told him as he readied the needles.

"He is a… she?" Ben looked the dog in the eyes.

"Yep, she is," Mack smiled.

"She doesn't have a chip, so not sure where she's from. But that wound there on her side, that's a clean slice. If I'm not mistaken, it looks like they used a scalpel on her," Mack said with a worried look.

"A scalpel?" Ben asked, shocked. "Who the hell would do that to an innocent animal?"

"A sick one," Mack replied, adding, "I'm not one hundred percent sure, but I wouldn't discount it either. It's a relatively fresh cut. I would say today, maybe yesterday was the very latest that it happened. Luckily, she could reach it and keep it partially clean herself. But I'll clean the wound and put some glue on it. It should be good as new in a few days," Mack said as he got to work. "Hold her tight Ben. This will hurt like a bitch."

Ben talked softly to the dog, resting his head on hers. Trying to keep her calm, he could feel her muscles tensing up as if she was planning to bolt from the table.

The store was empty and long past closing time. Abbi turned the sign and locked the door. She made her way back to the examination room to see how things were going. She leaned against the door frame, not daring to speak a word for fear of scaring the dog. *The poor thing…* her brow knitted with concern. Mack was bent over the dog, gently cleaning the wound. Her eyes sought Ben. *He's a remarkable man.* She watched him standing head to head with the dog. Not too many men would even bother with it in the first place, let alone rest their head next to it. The dog let out an ear-splitting yelp right next to his head, yet he didn't flinch.

"All right, that's all I can do for her," Mack said, straightening up. "I'll run into the house and get her some antibiotics, just in case," he said, washing his hands. Grabbing some paper towels, he noticed Abbi standing there. "Hey Abbi, anyone come in?" He asked, drying his hands off.

"Nope. I turned the sign around to closed, and locked the door for you," she said, slipping her hands into her jeans pockets.

"Good, good. I'm just going to run to the house, be right back," he said, leaving the room.

"A girl, is she?" Abbi smiled as she came into the room. At Ben's nod, she asked, "How's she doing? Will she be okay?"

"Yeah. Mack gave her some shots to get her up to date. He checked for a chip and there isn't one." He smiled at that, which immediately was replaced with a look of concern. "Ah, however, her wound... Mack thinks, it's fresh from this morning or yesterday, he can't be certain."

"Is it a bite?" Abbi asked.

"No," he said frowning, shaking his head. "Mack's not sure, but he thinks it looks like someone cut he with a scalpel."

"Oh my God, that's terrible!" Abbi cried. "Who the hell would do such a thing?" she asked in a horrified whisper.

"My sentiments exactly," he nodded in agreement, scratching the dog's chin. "Abbi, there's something I have to tell..." Ben was cut off by Mack's return.

"Here you go, guys. I wrote the instructions on the envelope. Just keep her quiet for a few days. I know she's dirty but don't let her get wet, at least not for a day or two," he said, handing the medication over to Ben. "I'll put some feelers out there, see if anyone is missing a dog."

"Thanks, Mack, if she doesn't have a home, I think she will have a new one in no time," Abbi said, rubbing the dog's head. "Yes, you do, you sweet thing you," Abbi crooned, planting a kiss on her nose. She wrapped her arms around the dog's chest while Ben took the rear and together, they set her on the floor.

"Come on. You two need a good night's sleep," she said to both man and dog.

"Thanks, Mack," Ben called out as he followed Abbi and the dog back to the car.

"No problem." Mack waved. "Glad I could help," he called out from the doorstep.

All three settled in the car for the ride back to Abbi's.

"Wow, I can't believe how tired I am," Ben said, wiping his eyes.

"It's been quite a day," she murmured in agreement, pulling into her laneway. Shutting the car off, she looked at him. "What was it you were meaning to tell me back at Mack's?" She asked.

"Oh. Right! Yeah, just something I wanted to run by you. It can wait until we get in the house," he yawned loudly.

She laughed at him. "I think it can wait until tomorrow. What do you think?"

He looked deeply into her eyes. He didn't want to put any fear into those beautiful orbs tonight. Nodding in agreement, he said, "Yeah, tomorrow will be soon enough."

Walking up the path to her house, Ben said, "So, I was thinking, how's Molly sound for a name?" he asked lightly.

She giggled. He just couldn't help himself. "I think Molly is a perfect name for her," she smiled, unlocking the door.

"Maybe just stay here with her for a bit and I'll get her some food and bring Brutus. We'll introduce them out here before letting her in the house," Abbi suggested.

"Right, good idea," he agreed, sitting down heavily on the top step. He could hear the dogs carrying on inside. Brutus was scratching at the door to get out. Seconds later, they emerged from the house. Brutus was in a harness with a muzzle covering his mouth. Abbi passed Ben a bowl of dog food. He took it from her, holding it until Brutus settled down.

"Just in case," Abbi explained at Ben's questioning look. "I never know how he will react most times."

Brutus playfully lunged at Molly. He seemed to decide that she was a friend and not a foe with the first sniff of her rear end. He quietly sat down next to her while she dug into the food.

"What about Lucy? How do you think she will react?" Ben asked, stroking both dogs.

"Lucy is laid back. She loves any animal that I've brought into the house, she'll be fine." She waved his concern away. "Well," Abbi said as she headed to the door, "do you want anything to eat or drink?"

"I never thought, did you need anything from your place?" She glanced at him, stopping at the door.

"Now that you mention it, yeah, I should have grabbed a change of clothes," he said, standing. "Care to go for a moonlit walk with me?" he asked, running his hand through his hair.

"Certainly," she smiled. "Just let me get Lucy. She could use the walk, too."

Ben was waiting in the yard for them, holding Brutus' leash.

"Do you think Molly will stay or should I grab a leash for her, too?" Abbi called to him, her hand on the doorknob.

He made a face. "I don't think she needs one, she's stayed with us since we found her."

Nodding, she closed the door and bounded down the steps. "Okay, I'll keep Brutus leashed for now, at least. Maybe on the way back, I'll let him run," she said, joining him in the yard.

She took his hand, tingling at the warmth of his touch as they headed towards his house. She had concerns about the next few days ahead of them. Her kids would arrive in three days and she felt the need to warn him.

Clearing her throat, she said, "I know we touched on the topic about my kids..." she stopped, wondering how to tell him.

"Go on," he encouraged her.

"Well, there's Luke, Lane and Ava," she stopped again.

"Yeah?" he looked at her.

"I have to warn you, Luke will be fine with us... likely will encourage it," she smiled, knowing exactly what Luke would say. The smile fell from her face when she continued, "As for Lane and Ava... frankly, I'm worried about what they will say..." she wrinkled her brow, "... to you..." she trailed off.

They had just reached his yard. The motion light caught their movement, washing them in its glow.

Ben stopped. Letting go of her hand, he put his arm around her and gazed into her eyes. "Do you care what they say or what they think?" he asked softly.

"No! Not really. It's just neither of them has a filter, you know what I mean?" She sighed. "They don't care what they say to anyone. It doesn't matter who it is."

"Abbi don't worry about it. I'm man enough to handle whatever it is they can dish out," he said, stroking her back.

"I know you are. I just wanted to give you a heads-up, so you're not shocked, is all," she replied.

The thought saddened her. She could see them demanding that she stop seeing Ben. If they did, things would get ugly really quick. There was no way she'd give up her happiness for her grown, adult children who lived hundreds of miles away. Nope, not going to happen!

"What are you thinking about?" he murmured.

"Nothing," she said.

"I can tell when the gears are moving, Abbi, just by looking into your eyes," he grinned.

"Nothing!" she laughed, kissing him quickly on the lips. She ran away and up the steps as her laughter turned to giggles, which abruptly stopped.

"Right," he said, shaking his head, smiling as he followed her up the steps.

"Ben, what the hell is that?" she stood transfixed, pointing to the porch floor.

There was the pool of dried blood Molly was lying next to. Brutus and Lucy were curled up against her on either side. Now that he wasn't in a panic, he noticed how large it was. Looking at Molly and again at the stain, anger rose in him.

"Son of a bitch," he swore.

"You… you don't think that was from her, do you?" Abbi asked, horrified at the thought.

"It sure looks to be, considering she was bleeding when we found her and it's about the same size as her." Crouching down, he looked at Molly's fur splayed out around her. Looking at the stain, he noticed how the same pattern was feathering out from the stain. "To think, she was out here, bleeding, when I was in there sleeping." He threw his hand towards the house in frustration. "If I find the bastard who did this to her, I'll wring his bloody neck." He stood up, covering his mouth with his hand.

She laid a hand on his chest. "Ben, you can't think like that. You had no idea she was even around here," she reasoned with him. "Maybe Mack was mistaken, and she was cut by a wire,"

He took her hand and brought it to his mouth, not kissing it, but just holding it there. He looked at Abbi's face. Every emotion possible was displayed on her soft features. He let out a sigh and said, "You're right. It could have been anything."

In his heart, he knew differently. Yes, he had jumped to conclusions today, more than once. But his gut was telling him that this wasn't the case. Did someone do this to Molly, just to drop her off on his property as a warning or was it only a coincidence? Whatever it was, he dared not tell Abbi tonight. Tomorrow was soon enough.

CHAPTER 16

He took his keys out of his pocket and unlocked the door, pushing it wide for Abbi to enter.

"Come on guys," he called to the dogs, closing the door. "Do you think I could chance a quick shower?" he asked Abbi, tossing his keys on the island. Looking down at his clothes, he noticed the Molly's blood smeared on his jeans.

"I guess you could try, but you will have to take that brace off," she replied, looking out the window. She could see the lights through the trees of her house. "Why don't you gather what you need and just take one at my place?" she offered. Turning she looked at him. "That way, we can get the dogs settled and I can help you if need be," she suggested quietly.

"Sure, I'll just grab a few things and we can leave," he said, going into his bedroom.

"Hey! Did you ever get those curtains hung?"

"Um… well, sort of," he chuckled. "Come, have a look."

She walked into the hall that would lead to his bedroom. Standing at the door, she leaned against the frame. "Wow!" she laughed, walking to the window. "How creative," she said, smiling as she fingered the garbage bags taped to the window frame.

"Yeah, I thought so, too," he laughed, shutting a drawer.

He stuffed a change of clothes and good grief, pajama bottoms in a backpack. Normally he slept in the raw but not tonight. He didn't think Abbi would approve.

"I'll be right back," he tossed over his shoulder as he walked out of the room.

She turned to mumble, "Hmm…" Her eyes caught the bed in the center of the room, the covers lay back where he tossed them. She could picture in her mind, him lying there. The rise and fall of his chest with every breath he took. *He'd look like an angel… no… a God…*

In the bathroom, he collected his toothbrush, deodorant, and body wash and sauntered back to his room. Abbi was off in a trance again he noticed.

Staring at my bed, is she? He grinned, shaking his head.

"Abbi, you ready to go?" he asked, zipping up the bag. "Abbi!" A smile playing on his lips.

She just about jumped out of her skin. "What?" she said, matching his tone

"I'm ready to go, are you?" he said, slinging the pack on his shoulder.

"Yes, yes, of course!" She hurried to the hallway.

Ben followed her through to the kitchen. He rather enjoyed following her; she gave off such a nice view.

She looked over her shoulder and caught him eyeing her.

"Do you have everything?"

At his nod, she called the dogs. Opening the door to let them outside, she snagged hold of Brutus' leash.

"Yeah, I think so," he replied, grabbing his keys. He locked and closed the door firmly behind him.

As they started off, Abbi glanced at him.

"What will you do about that stain on the porch?"

"Ah, I haven't really thought about it honestly. Hopefully, a couple of coats of paint will cover it. Which it needs anyway since the BBQ caught fire."

"True. I can give you a hand if you like," she offered. "There's a power washer in my shed, buried under something I'm sure," she laughed.

Putting his arm around her shoulders, he said softly, "I'll tell you what. You help me with my porch, and I'll help you clean out your shed."

"Deal," she said. "I would shake on it, but your hands are busy," she chuckled as they stepped into her yard.

"I'll do one better." He moved his hand to the back of her head, bent towards her, searching out her lips with his own. He gently kissed her, feeling her arms go around his waist, he deepened the kiss. On any other night, he could have stayed right there kissing her, but this wasn't any normal night.

Breaking for air, he whispered, "As much as I would love to stand here kissing your sweet lips till dawn, Abbi, I'm exhausted. Let's get in the house before I curl up here in the bushes and pass out," he yawned loudly.

"You started it," she accused.

Nodding he smiled. "Right, I did. And so, you know, I plan on finishing it," he said as they climbed the stairs. "Just not tonight." He sent her a wink.

She unlocked the door; Brutus shoved it wide with his nose.

"Do you still want that shower?" she looked at him, locking the door.

"If you don't mind giving me a hand, I would," he said, looking up as he set his bag on the table.

"Um, sure." Remembering what Doc had said about the pain, she asked, "Are you needing any pain meds yet?"

"Please. The freezing is long gone, makes me regret stopping you from getting the prescription," he said with a tight smile.

"If you want to head to the bathroom, I'll bring them to you. I'm just going to put on the kettle. Do you want a cup of hot chocolate?"

He noticed her rambling on. "Sure, that will be great," he said, heading to the bathroom.

You can do this, Abbi... She tried to reassure herself. *Sure, I can! I just haven't seen a man naked for... Oh... four years. No big deal.* Oh, but it was. It was a huge deal. She took the kettle, filling it with water. She sat it on the stove and switched it on. Ben wasn't any ordinary man; he was all muscle. *His arms are strong, the veins standing out against his skin... and his skin is soft, like butter. A lovely, defined chest with a light scattering of hair that trailed over his stomach... Oh my! His abs were one glorious ripple after another. The soft dusting of hair around his navel, dropped below his waistband.* Her eyes yet to see where it ended.

Girl, what is wrong with you?? Why did you just have to think about that now, when you have to go in there and help him!

"Abbi, Luv, are you coming?" he called out from the bathroom.

She grabbed the bottle of pain meds. "Ah, yeah, be right there!" She took a deep steadying breath, grabbing his bag off the table. She walked on shaky legs to the bathroom. She stopped just outside the open door, peeking through the gap between the door and the frame. There he was, sitting on the closed lid of the toilet. His head in his hand, fully clothed. Her heart went out to him. He looked utterly spent. She moved so she could peek around the edge of the door. In response, the floor creaked at that very moment, causing him to jerk his head in her direction. He caught her standing there with only one eye looking at him.

A bubble of laughter rose in his chest. "What exactly are you doing?"

"I… ahh… nothing," she said, walking into the bathroom. "I'll just start the shower for you." She turned it on and adjusted the temperature. Turning back, she saw that he was now standing, swaying in place. She rushed to his side. "Here, let me get this sling off for you." Going around his back to untie it.

"God, that's a relief." He slowly rotated his head.

She stayed behind him, holding his shirt as he pulled his arm out. She tugged it over his head, tossing it to the floor. Looking at the brace, she said worriedly, "Are you sure about this Ben? I don't know if I'll be able to figure out how to take it off, let alone put it back on..."

"There's a strap there, just pull on it, the one that goes around my chest, and another one on my arm, just below my shoulder. Do you see it?" he asked.

She answered by pulling on the strap under his arm, hearing a tearing sound as she did. She did the same with the strap on his shoulder, allowing it to slip off easily. His back was just as well defined as the front of him, which brought her gaze to the waist of his pants.

"Um, I'll just reach around you here and undo your pants for you, okay?"

"Yeah, that will be fine," he replied. This was about to get very interesting, he smirked.

She unbuttoned his pants and pulled on the zipper when the damned thing got caught. She tugged and tugged but it wouldn't budge. Going around to the front of him, she tried again.

"What is it?" He had to bite his lip; otherwise he'd laugh in her face.

"The zipper is... stuck." She pushed her hair out of her face. "Hang on, I'll just grab a bar of soap." She took the bar from the shower and rubbed it on the zipper. "Got it! Now, sit down on the toilet so I can take your pants off," she told him, grabbing some towels from the shelf.

As tired as he was, he couldn't help teasing her. "Take my pants off... I rather like the sound of that." A mischievous glint lit his eyes.

She sat the towels on the counter giving him a sidelong glance. "Hmm, I bet you do. Lift your butt please."

Bracing himself against the wall, he did as he was told. She slipped his pants past his hips. She noticed the effort it took for him to do that as he resettled himself. Tugging on one pant leg she slipped it off, followed by the other, then his socks. Even his feet were perfect… Standing with her hands on her hips, all that was left were his briefs. *How the heck is this going to work?* … She gnawed at her bottom lip.

Standing up, he could see the look in her eyes, that look when she thought a lot. "Why don't you just put a towel around my waist until I get in?"

She pointed a finger at him. "Good idea!" She grabbed a towel wrapping it around him. "Now what?"

My God, it's getting hot in here…

Abbi pulled on her shirt rapidly to get some air flowing. That wasn't working. Ben watched in surprise when she grabbed the hem of her shirt, pulling it off in one fluid motion. Whipping it in a corner.

"Um, now I guess I'll just shimmy out of my, uh… shorts," he decided for a better word.

Throwing her hair up into a messy bun, she went to the shelf and grabbed a clip, securing it in place. Puzzled, she looked at his reflection in the mirror. "How are you going to do that with a towel wrapped around you and one good hand?"

She was right.

She was beautiful standing there looking at him. Her hair softly curling, now up, showed the graceful curve of her neck. He wanted to plant a kiss there but stopped himself.

"I'll just hold another towel up while you do that," she suggested, turning back towards him. Her eyes grew huge when she saw that the towel was now larger. She leaned back against the counter, blindly searching for the other towel that she had put there. Her fingers found it, finally. Snatching it up, she shook the folds from it. Holding it up, she turned her head to the door. "Hurry now, we need to get you to bed!" She made a grimace and bit her tongue. *Shut up, Abbi!*

"Right. I'll do that," he chuckled, shaking his head. *Damn, I have no self-control when I'm around her…*

He dropped the towel and took off his briefs. Moving the

shower curtain aside, he climbed in under the steaming water.

"You good?" She wasn't waiting for his response. "Okay, I'll make the hot chocolate now." Taking the pain meds out of her pocket, she shook two in her hand, sticking her hand behind the curtain. "Here are the pills."

"Thanks. Just drop them, Luv."

He opened his mouth under her hand, added some water from the shower and swallowed as he heard her make a hasty retreat. Hopefully, the pills kicked in fast. He stood there for a good three minutes, just turning slowly in circles. It felt wonderful on his sore muscles. He pumped shampoo one-handed and slapped it on his head, just as he heard Abbi returning.

"Are you doing good in there?" she called out.

"Not too bad, just scrubbing my hair right now."

"Nice, I have your bag here, need anything out of it?"

"Yeah, could you get me the body wash, please?" he asked.

She stuck her hand in, holding the bottle out to him. "Grab that puff thing there and I'll squirt some on it for you."

"The what?" he asked with amusement in his voice.

"The pink thing hanging there on the hook, you know, a puff?"

"Never heard of it before," he said, holding it out for the body wash. "Usually I just dump it in my hand and rub it all over my body."

Thanks, I really needed that visual. All over your wet, glistening body.

The sound of him hissing made her come back to the moment at hand.

"What's wrong?" she asked.

"Nothing just rubbed a little too hard on my shoulder, is all."

"Okay, let me know when you're done, and I'll get the towel ready for you."

The water shut off the second the words were out of her mouth.

"Wait, a minute! I'm not ready!"

He could hear her scrambling. Something crashed to the floor.

Smiling to himself, he waited for her to give the all-clear.

Breathlessly she said, "Okay, go ahead."

He moved the curtain aside and stepped out of the shower. He took the one end of the towel, wrapping it behind him as she held the other end. She risked a glance at him to see if he was covered. Finding that he was, she wrapped the other end around him, tucking the corner in.

"There. It's perfect. I'll show you the spare bedroom now. You can put your stuff in there and get dressed..." she trailed off.

He followed her out and down the hall. She pointed to the left.

"That's my library, where I do all of my writing." Moving along, she pointed to the left again. "The mongrels' room is that one." Stopping, she flicked the light on to see the three dogs lying there sound asleep. Brutus and Lucy were lying beside Molly again as if they were giving her their strength. Turning the light off, she continued onward. She turned to the right where there was another short hallway with two doors across from each other. She opened the first one on the left. "This one is mine," she said, flicking on the light switch.

Ben's brows shot up in surprise. A huge four-poster bed sat in the center, not against a wall, but in the center of the room. A sheer, brown curtain from corner to corner draped across the top, dipping in the middle. The same material trailed down all four columns of the bed to the floor. The bed was covered in a quilt with wildflowers etched on it. The bedroom walls were soft green and a white wicker set sat under one window. Across the room, facing the lake, there was a bay window with plump pillows scattered for seating. He could picture Abbi sitting there on a rainy day, a book in her hands. The whole room screamed, earthy.

"I know. It's a little over the top, but it's my dream bedroom," she said shyly.

"No! Not at all, Abbi, it's you," he murmured, brushing her hair out of her eyes.

She wanted to kiss him for his understanding but remembered

he only wore the towel. She needed more clothes between them, more than a towel that could slip off at a moment's notice. She smiled instead.

"And this here is the spare room," she said, taking a few steps away from her door.

Pushing the door open on the right, she walked into the room over to the bed and pulled the blankets back. Ben saw a queen-sized bed, the head, pushed up against the wall. A floral quilt covered it with plump pillows resting on the headboard. A lamp on the dresser cast a soft glow over the room. The low window gave a view to the lake from the bed. He could picture what it would look like come morning, watching it come alive with the first beam of sunrise hitting the lake.

Nodding towards a door, Abbi said, "There is a connecting bathroom there to my room."

Ben looked back into the hall for the door to the bathroom.

Knowing what he was looking for, she told him, "You only can access it from our rooms."

"Huh, that's cool."

"Yeah, it was actually another bedroom, but I liked the idea of having a private bath back here," she said, sliding the pocket door open for him to step in.

"My room is through there," she motioned at the door directly across from his bathroom door.

"Wow!" Ben was floored by what he saw. The wall that faced the lake was a solid pane of glass from floor to ceiling. Two steps took you up to an oval-shaped tub large enough for two people. He stood looking at the wall of glass, squinting.

"Ah..." he pointed to the bathtub, "... aren't you afraid of someone seeing you while you bathe?" he asked, tilting his head to look at her.

She laughed. "Everyone who's seen it asks the same thing. No, it's one-sided glass, like the cops use."

"Good to know, otherwise, I thought it brazen of you," he

grinned, chuckling.

She turned around. "The shower is over there and the toilet and vanity through there," she pointed, showing him the doorway.

"This is gorgeous," he said, looking around in awe.

"Thanks! I designed it myself."

"Even more impressive," he nodded, a look of admiration in his eyes.

He made her smile at that. She walked back to his room.

"So, if you want to get… dressed, I'll go get your brace. Do you think you can handle it?" *Please say yes.*

"Yeah, I should be fine," he said, looking around.

"Crap, we forgot your bag. I'll get it too. Do you want your drink brought in here?" she asked.

"That would be great, thanks." He wanted nothing more than to sit up all night talking to her, but reality was kicking him in the ass. He needed sleep, and he needed it now… He sat down heavily on the side of the bed.

Abbi took off down the hall to collect his bag, grab his brace and their drinks that were likely cold by now. She picked up his clothes and quickly ran them into the laundry room, spraying the dried blood with a stain remover. She threw them in the washer and started it. Going into the bathroom, she grabbed up his bag, slung it over her shoulder, tucked his brace under her arm and picked up their cups. Making a mental note, she needed to tell him to remind her to get his pills at the pharmacy tomorrow as she headed back to him.

"So, hey…. Oh…!" she said softly, her eyes instantly matching her tone.

He had fallen asleep. Flat on his back, his legs dangled over the edge. The towel had slipped, revealing skin from hip to thigh.

Sweet baby Jesus… She sucked in a ragged breath, biting her lip. She had work to do. She couldn't leave him all night to sleep in a wet towel.

Chapter 17

Thankfully, that's all it had revealed. She wasn't entirely sure if she could contain herself if it hadn't. Of course, you could... stop acting like a sex-deprived fool! Well, she was sex deprived, but not enough to take advantage of him.

She tiptoed to the dresser and quietly sat the cups down along with the brace. She watched him as she eased his bag off her shoulder. Sitting it on the floor, she slowly unzipped it, pawing through it until she found his pajama pants. She'd forgo the underwear; the pants would be challenging enough. She approached the bed, holding onto them. *How am I going to do this without waking him up...?*

He really was a work of art. Her eyes ran over his body from head to... she gulped. At least the important part was covered. Smooth skin stretched across his hip and groin area to his thigh. *Enough Abbi! Get the man's pants on and let him sleep...*

Bending to slip the waistband over one foot then the other, she slid them up to his thighs without so much as a twitch from him. Now, all she had to do was shimmy the rest up to his waist. She gripped the waistband so hard her knuckles turned white. Inch by inch they slid upwards, under the towel. She took a quick glance at his face to see if he was awake and watching her. Thankfully, he wasn't. She got as far as his thighs. She hissed out the breath she was holding. Taking a deep breath, she eased onto the bed, straddling his thighs with hers; she dared not sit on him. Getting a firm grip on the pants once again, she checked his face for a sign that he was awake. She slowly pulled them upwards... She was silently congratulating herself until she met with resistance.

For cripe's sake, they're stuck!!! On his butt and other things, she noticed. She pushed down with the back of her hands into the mattress as she gripped the waist. *Just need to get them over this beautiful ass...* She grunted aloud. Stifling a giggle, she quickly looked at his face and saw he was still fast asleep. Straightening up on her knees, she leaned back, putting her hands on her hips to study her work.

Just then, Ben woke up. She froze, hoping he didn't see her and would fall back asleep. He did, thank God!

She gently grabbed the waist again, leaning forward she eased them up past his... she looked down. Her eyes fell on his... package. One that the towel still covered.

She had a vivid image of face planting onto him. A horrified look settled on her features. In one swift movement, she yanked the pants up to his waist and tugged on the towel. Damn it! Now the towel was stuck under him. *That would be because he is laying on it, you fool!* She stumbled to stand on the floor.

"Abbi, what... where...?" he stopped.

"Sorry about that," she motioned. "I didn't want to leave you laying in a wet towel all night." She couldn't help but blush. "Um, now that you're awake, we really should put the brace back on." She hurriedly snatched it from the dresser.

"Sure, maybe it will help. I'm having some doubts about that," he replied in pain.

She handed him a cup. "Here, it's still warm, drink up while I do this."

He took a sip while she slipped the brace over his hand and up to his shoulder. Reaching around his back, she fastened it, making sure it was snug.

"There, how does that feel?" she asked, tugging at it.

"Better, thanks." he gave her a sleepy smile. Ben sat his cup on the bedside table and crawled up to rest against the pillows. "Lay with me, please. I promise nothing will happen."

The look in his eyes made it impossible for her to say no. Nodding her head, she laid down facing him.

"What time is it?" He yawned.

"Good question." Pulling her cell out of her back pocket she said, "Um, it's 11:30." She noticed five missed calls. She swiped the screen to see the call log, thinking it was one of her kids. She frowned.

Ben was watching her. "What is it?"

"Oh, nothing. Just a few missed calls," she said, turning away to set her phone on the table. She turned back towards him. "What?" she asked.

He had propped his arm under his head and was staring at her. "Nothing," he mumbled. He loved watching her. The light from the glow of the lamp played over her features. He worried about what was going on. He was on the verge of telling her, but now wasn't the time. Not here, not now.

Abbi was watching him, too. Watched his brow wrinkle in thought. *What is he thinking about...?* She reached a hand to smooth out the lines on his brow.

"You look so tired," she softly murmured, her hand slipping into his hair. She ran her fingers through it, noticing how soft it felt to the touch. Everything on him was soft. She trailed her hand down the side of his face to his cheek.

"I am," he said, turning his face to kiss her palm.

She felt a little fire spark from his lips to her hand, down her arm, flaring throughout her body. He turned his head, looking into her eyes. She moved her head closer, planting a soft kiss on his lips. She leaned back against the pillows, and opening her arms, she whispered, "Come here."

That was all Ben needed to hear. He slipped his good arm under her as she guided his head to her chest, the other in the brace resting across her stomach. She breathed in his masculine scent. Her lips grazed his forehead as she stroked his back. Ben felt his eyes drifting shut, felt her fingers tracing softly over his bare skin, her lips touching his forehead. Despite his exhaustion, his body reacted to her touch. Sadly, he was too tired to reciprocate. The beat of her heart, lulling him to sleep. He heard her softly croon, 'sleep now my darling' as his eyes drifted closed in exhaustion.

Something was crawling on Ben. He opened his eyes to see Abbi's neck in front of him. Her hair was covering her face, tickling his nose. He leaned forward, brushing a kiss against her soft skin. He could feel her pulse beating steadily beneath his lips, he darted his tongue out to taste her sweetness. She moaned softly in her sleep, gathering him closer to her. His reaction was instant. He wanted nothing more than to take her into his arms and make sweet love to her while slowly watching her body awaken with desire. He gently eased away, watching her as he did so. Untangling himself from her embrace, he touched his lips to hers before slipping out of the bed. He would let the dogs out and make her breakfast, he decided, heading to the bathroom.

Abbi woke slowly, reaching out to seek Ben only to find the bed empty. Feeling disappointed, she thought about last night. She had lain awake for a bit after he had fallen asleep, just holding him in her arms. She loved the weight of him on her. His soft breathing with every rise and fall of his chest. Reaching for her cell, she looked to see the time... 8:30... she groaned. Getting up, she stumbled into the bathroom. She did her business and jumped in to take a quick shower. Turning the taps off, she could hear the dogs barking outside. She hurried to get dressed in her room, throwing on a tank top and sweatpants. She tugged on a zip-up sweater with

'Canada' emblazoned across her chest. As she slipped her bare feet into some fuzzy slippers, she made her way into the hall. Following the scent of bacon coming from the kitchen, she found Ben standing at the stove, bare-chested in his pajama pants.

"Morning, Luv. I've fed the gang; the dogs are outside just now." He smiled at her. "I hope you don't mind me cooking?" he asked, pouring her a cup of coffee.

She took it from him, smiling her thanks. She glanced at the table to see that he had set it. "Not at all. I could get used to this." She motioned with her cup, tossing him a grin. "How's your shoulder feeling?" she asked, setting her coffee down on the counter. She walked over to him, making sure the brace was still snug.

He turned towards her, "Better, I think. I needed that sleep," he said, slipping his arm around her waist, pulling her close. "Thank you, Abbi, for taking care of me." He glanced at her lips before bending his head to kiss her. Cradling her head in his hand, he tilted her head back, laying quick kisses along her jawline before dropping a soft one on her lips.

The toaster popped just then. She slid her hands down his bare chest, trailing her nails against his skin, watching in awe as goosebumps sprung to the surface. "Are you cold?" she asked, buttering the toast.

"No, Abbi. I'm not cold; it's just what you do to me. You really have no idea, do you?"

She glanced at him over her shoulder. "Um, a little. Maybe. I still have my doubts about… you."

"Seriously…. How could you think that? Do you take me for the type of man to go around kissing just anyone?" Annoyed, he walked to the table, setting the plate of bacon on it. Pulling out a chair he sat, brooding. "Why don't you believe me?"

"Look, Ben." She began "It's not that I don't think you have feelings for me or that I don't believe you. I know that you do. It's just…"

"It's just what, Abbi?

She brought the plate of toast to the table along with a jug of orange juice. Sitting down, she turned her chair towards him, looking him in the eyes. "It's just…" *Stop worrying about it and tell him…*. "It's just," she cleared her throat. "I'm ashamed… of my body." She cast her eyes around the room before settling them on a spot on the floor. She dared not look him in the eyes.

Well, that shocked the hell out of him. He was sure she'd say she was too old again. For the life of him, he couldn't possibly think why she'd be ashamed.

She could see the puzzlement play over his face.

"Of what?" he asked, dumbfounded.

CHAPTER 18

"Ben, I had three kids... two being twins." She waited for him to clue in.

His brows shot up. Tilting his head, his eyes round, he spat out, "So?"

She closed her eyes and rubbed her forehead. "I have stretch marks and scars, OK? I was huge when I was pregnant with the boys... 16 years old and my body has been ruined ever since." She opened her eyes, needing to see his reaction. Ava was also born by c-section, so not only was I cut once... but twice."

She watched his face soften with understanding.

"Abbi... Luv." He took her hand in his, bringing it to his lips,

"Your body doesn't define who you are." Squinting in disbelief, he asked, "Do you honestly think I would judge you for it?"

"Well… No. I suppose not. But you meet gorgeous women every day." She dashed away the tears that sprang to her eyes. She stood up, pacing the floor. "I can't compete with someone with smooth uncut, wrinkle-free skin."

"You don't have to compete with anyone Abbi. You have my heart… please, don't ever for a minute forget it," he said earnestly. Catching her hand, he dragged her onto his lap. Turning her face towards him, he kissed her, convincing her his words were true.

"What the hell is that?" Ben asked pulling away.

"Huh? What do you mean?" she asked, breathlessly.

He motioned with his hand towards the hall. "That… it sounds like a rooster. Do you have one of those I've yet to meet?" he laughed at the thought.

"Oh! It's my phone!!" Jumping up, she took off down the hall to the spare bedroom. Grabbing it from the bedside table, she answered it with a breathless, "Hello?"

Ben was making a bacon sandwich, squirting ketchup on it, as she came back into the room. He glanced up when he heard her saying, "Hello… I can't hear you… is anyone there?"

Shrugging her shoulders, she hit the end button.

"Who was it?" he inquired, biting into his sandwich.

She shook her head. "I'm not sure. It was unknown caller again." Sitting down, she snatched a piece of bacon. Thoughtfully she said, "Someone was there, I could hear them breathing."

Ben's suspicions were back. "Right," he nodded. "Okay. I was so tired last night. I can't remember if I mentioned this to you or not." He took a sip of his juice. "I think something is going on here, Abbi."

She darted a look at him. "Going on as in…?" she asked, biting the bacon in half.

Taking a deep breath, he said, "At first I thought maybe the paparazzi had found out I was living here."

"Hmm, go on" she motioned with her hand for him to continue.

"You remember the night Mark was over at my place?" At her nod, he continued. "When we kissed on your porch… I had the feeling we weren't alone," he trailed off.

"How so?" she asked with a frown, licking the grease from her fingers. "The dogs would have sensed someone out there," she pointed out smacking her lips.

"That's what I thought. But the feeling was there all the same. I even sat for a spell outside, thinking I might hear or see something."

Her brows shot up. *So that's why he stayed so long...* Now she felt foolish thinking he was pining away for her. She laughed at the memory of it.

"I'm serious…"

She put her hand up. "I know, I know. I'm laughing at something else." She waved her hand, dismissing it. "The trees around here can make you think you see something when it's not really there." She gathered the dishes and walked to the counter. "Plus, the lake carries sound, causing an echo off of them." She pointed a dirty fork in his direction. "Take, for instance, the day I was cleaning my windows. I heard your music playing loud and clear over here… and then when I tripped on the last step and fell flat on my face? I heard you laughing at me." She smiled as she loaded the dishwasher. "Which wasn't very nice of you, I might add."

My God, it isn't the paparazzi at all. It's her they are after…

"Abbi." He sat there, drumming the table with his fingers.

Glancing at him, she said, "Yeah?" She saw his face had lost all color. Was he feeling sick suddenly? "What is it?"

"I haven't played music, nor did I laugh at you. The only time that I've seen you trip was the day I caught you in Mack's store."

She stood there shaking her head in denial. "No, no, no, that… that just can't be."

He got up and walked over to her, taking her by the arms.

"Abbi listen to me. The phone calls..." He threw his hand towards the lake. "The boat no less than a hundred feet from your shore... the laughing and music... I promise you that wasn't me." He licked his lips. "What if what happened to Molly was done on purpose..."

She started to squawk.

"No, hear me out." He put a finger to her lips. "Mack said it looked like she was cut with a scalpel, not a knife or a piece of wire, but a scalpel... He's a retired Veterinarian. I'm confident he'd know the difference." God, he hated doing this to her.

She shook her head. "But why would someone hurt her if they were after me? That just makes little sense." Deep down she had a feeling he was right, about everything except Molly. *What kind of person could do such a thing to a defenseless animal?*

Ben sighed. "A warning for me."

She jerked her head up, looking deeply into his eyes.

"To stay away from you..." he answered quietly. "What happened to the guy that was stalking you? Did you go to the police about him?" he asked softly.

Nodding her head, "I did. And I had a restraining order put on him. After that, he left me alone." She suddenly felt a cold shiver run down her spine at the memory of it.

Ben swore as he took a step back, shoving his hand through his hair. "I'm sorry." He pulled her into his arms as she started to shiver uncontrollably. "It's okay," he soothed quietly.

"Maybe it's all just a coincidence. That's likely what it is," she said against his chest.

"Coincidence or not I'm calling the police." He rubbed her back. "Do you recall his name?" He hated to put her through this but had little choice.

"Ah, yeah. It was... Um, Jacob?" She rubbed her forehead. It was suddenly pounding and for the life of her, she couldn't remember his last name. She pulled herself out of the safety of his arms. "Um, I have to look on my computer for his last name," she said woodenly, walking to the library.

Ben watched her with concern. He'd follow her shortly, as soon as he called the dogs in and locked the door.

Abbi was sitting at her computer, staring blankly at the screen when Ben joined her.

"Hey, Luv." No response. Taking a chair, he watched her face as he sat beside her. She didn't say a word, just kept staring at the computer screen. He gazed at her profile. Reaching for her chin he turned her gently to face him.

"Abbi. Luv look at me," he murmured.

She did. The look she gave him tore his heart out. Her once beautiful, sparkling eyes were despondent. He stood up taking her hand in his; the call to the police could wait. Tugging her away from the desk, he guided her to the couch. Sitting, he pulled her onto his lap. Taking a throw blanket, he spread it over them. Ben wrapped her in his arms as she collapsed on his chest. He could feel her body wrack with sobs as he rubbed her back soothingly.

"It's okay sweet one. I'm here. Let it all out." he crooned in hushed tones, holding her tight. "No one will ever hurt you again."

Slowly her body melted into his, her sobs turning into the odd sniffle.

He reached for a box of tissues from the table, holding it while she took a handful. Mopping her face, she dabbed his chest too. With a shaky laugh, she stated, "I always seem to cry on you."

"That's okay… I don't mind."

She looked up at him, her eyes were red from crying. She laid a soft hand on his face, locking her eyes with his. "What did I ever do to deserve you?" Holding onto his face for dear life, she gently placed a kiss on his lips as fresh tears threatened again.

He groaned when he felt her tongue dance with his. *God, she is pure torture…* His arousal was immediate when she turned to straddle his thighs. He could feel her hands running down his chest, down further to his stomach, causing him to tighten it at her touch. Leaning his head back, he broke the kiss off, fully intending to stop. He felt her hot wet tongue trail down his neck, lapping and tasting at his throat, her teeth nipping him there. Hissing out a breath, he grabbed her hands that were fast approaching the waistband of his pajama pants. Holding onto them, he looked into her desire filled eyes, seeing the same raw emotion he knew that was in his own.

"Are you sure this is what you want?" he asked softly.

She leaned forward gazing intently into his eyes, coming closer inch by inch until their noses touched. "I have never been surer of anything in my life, Ben," she murmured against his lips.

He placed his hands under her thighs holding onto them, hiking her closer. Using his good hand to cradle her bottom as their lips clung to one another. There was no question in either of their minds where this was leading them. He stood up, lifting her as he did. She wrapped her legs around his waist as he carried her to her bedroom. Devouring her with his mouth, as he gently laid her on the bed. Pulling the clip from her hair, he ran his fingers through the softness of it as he covered her body with his. His mouth trailed hot kisses below her ear.

A soft whimper escaped past her parted lips as she felt him unzip her sweater, tugging it off one arm then the other, his lips never leaving her skin. His mouth left a blazing trail as he brushed the tops of her breasts, just above her tank top.

She needed to touch him, or she'd go insane. She trailed her hands across his back, through his hair, as she felt his sweet mouth taste her skin.

Ben reached for the hem of her shirt, slowly edging it upwards. He felt Abbi's hands grab him, stopping him from removing it. He looked up at her, seeing the slight shake of her head. He slid up to look her in the eyes, his gaze dropping to her lips.

Softly he murmured, "Abbi, my sweet one." He nibbled on her bottom lip. "When we make love..." he paused, slipping his tongue in to plunder her mouth. Pulling slowly away he looked into her eyes again, "I'll make love to every inch of your beautiful body," he stated, dipping his head as he sucked on her earlobe.

She groaned, nodding her head. This time when he reached for the hem of her shirt, she didn't stop him. For the life of her, she couldn't stop him even if she wanted to.

He slowly pulled it up, stopping at her bra where he laid a soft kiss just below the band that rested against her ribcage. Straddling her legs, he peeled it off the rest of the way. "Am I too heavy for you, Luv?" he asked, concern in his eyes.

She couldn't respond. Instead, she vigorously shook her head no.

He bent down to kiss her mouth once, before he made his descent down her body.

He hooked a finger into her bra strap, dragging it down as he trailed his mouth onto new territory. He reached behind her back and in one deft motion he was tugging her bra off.

Abbi closed her eyes, her hands clenching the blanket beneath her when she felt his mouth tugging and suckling. A heavy fiery wetness came over her, exploding to her most private core. She ran her hands through his hair, holding him fast to her, feeling his mouth dip down her ribcage to her belly, just above the waistband of her pants. *Okay ... this is it. One look at my stretch marks and he will hightail it out of here... sure, they were long faded, but they were still there damn it!!*

His fingers gripped the waistband with one hand as the other trailed from her stomach down her leg. Pulling them down, he replaced them with his hands, gliding them over her inner thighs. He touched his mouth softly to the lines that would forever mar her body. He didn't care. They could cover her from head to toe and he'd still want her as much as he did at this very moment.

She tensed. Any second he will jump up and run for home. She clenched her eyes closed... waiting for the heat of his body to leave her.

Yep, there he goes... She felt the cool air on her skin where the warmth of his body had been just a few moments ago. She slowly opened one eye to see him gazing down at her. She lifted her head to see what he was looking at. *Well, at least my bra and underwear matched...*

"I'll be right back." He bounded off the bed, leaving the room.

She knew it. There was no way he'd be back now. She pulled the corner of the quilt, covering herself from head to toe. She needed to wallow in self-pity before she had to face him again, if ever. She heard a rustling sound. Ignoring it, she laid as still as she could.

"I'm back…. Abbi? Where did you go?"

Looking at the bed he saw that she was gone. He looked in the bathroom to find it empty. It took him seconds to cross the hall to search in his bag for a condom. He looked at the bed again when he noticed her hair peeking out from above the quilt. He walked over to the bed and sat down, pulling the corner away as he did so.

"What are you doing?" He chuckled.

She opened her eyes, looking at him with sadness. "I know the sight of me turned you off," she mumbled.

He let out a bark of laughter, one brow raised in question. "Are you, insane woman?"

"Well, why else would you leave after staring at me?" She motioned to her stomach.

His eyes darkened with passion. "I was staring at you because I'm in awe of you. You're stunning Abbi," he breathed. "And… I left to get this." He held up the package, shaking it. His head tilted to the side, a small smirk on his glorious lips.

Her eyes grew large. "Oh!" She felt like a fool!

"Yeah," he said, smiling as he leaned over to kiss her.

The heaviness returned to her at the touch of his lips. Wrapping her hands behind his neck, she pulled him down beside her.

His hand found her breast, his thumb flicking softly the tight bud that had formed there. He groaned deep in his throat. *If I don't stop this sweet torture soon, I'll be of no use to her...* Still sitting beside her on the bed, he pulled away, turning, so she was looking at his back. He bent towards her waist, tugging on her panties, sliding them down to her ankles. She helped by rapidly kicking them off.

Slowly, he ran his hands back up her calves, trailing kisses on her knees and thighs. His lips followed his hands, only stopping to slip one finger inside her, finding her dripping as he nipped her hip bone.

She bucked and moaned under his touch. *Lord have mercy, that was just his finger...* She cried out reaching for him, blindly grabbing his arm as she tugged him to her.

He crawled up beside her, laying his head next to hers. He kissed her then, so passionately; she thought she'd pass out from lack of air

Reaching out, she ran her hand down his stomach past his waistband, seeking his arousal. Her fingers lightly stroked its softness. She needed to feel him... feel him inside her before she lost all control.

Ben pulled back, grabbing her hand. "Careful my love," he whispered hotly against her lips.

"I can't... I... Ben, I can't wait any longer... please," she begged with a whimper. She tugged at his pants, pulling them down.

"Where did the condom go?" he asked, searching for it.

"It doesn't matter," she said, rapidly shaking her head as she pulled his pants off. *I just about fainted last night trying to put them on him, now I'm acting like a harlot to get them off...*

"Are you sure?" he asked surprised.

"Yes, damn it!" She shouted in frustration, pushing him back onto the pillows.

Ben laughed at her eagerness as she moved to straddle him. His laughter was immediately replaced with a low guttural moan as a liquid fire spread through his loins.

She rose and fell twice before he grabbed her by the waist,

turning her around to lay her on her back. She instinctively wrapped her legs around his hips, trying desperately to draw him closer.

He slowly withdrew. Just the tip still inside her warmth… waiting.

She clenched her legs, bringing her hips up to meet him, as he slowly pushed forward stroking inside her.

He withdrew again. Teasing her, marveling at the sounds coming from her throat. Sounds that were for him and him only. Until finally, he could no longer control himself. When she arched up to meet him this time, he grabbed her hips, thrusting deep inside. He felt her insides clench around him, knew that she was on the verge of climaxing from the sweet sounds coming from her throat, the shuddering pleasure coursing through her body.

With one last thrust, he brought them both over the edge of pure ecstasy. They soared together among the stars before coming down in quivering waves of spent pleasure. He collapsed on top of Abbi. Rolling over onto his back, he brought her with him. She lay there, softly nestled on his chest.

Abbi could hear his heartbeat slowly return to normal, as did her own. She was in awe of what they had just shared. She was utterly spent. Never in her life had she ever felt so alive, so loved, so respected, so like… jelly. She curled up against Ben. Sighing in contentment she started shivering; she didn't want to move just yet.

Ben titled his head, looking down at her. She was breathing softly. The gentle rise and fall of her chest told him she was sleeping.

He slowly took the quilt, covering them both with it. Pulling her tighter to him, he kissed her forehead. His shoulder hurt like a bitch, but it was worth it. He closed his eyes.

Later, when they woke, he'd see about getting that prescription that Doc had given him and call the police. With everything that is going on, *I need it to heal like yesterday…* he thought, falling off in a light slumber.

The person stumbled on a limb that had fallen from one of the trees that graced Abbi's property. They cursed as they fell along the shore of her backyard, splashing into the water. The focus had been on her house and not where they were walking. They needed to see what the couple inside were doing at that very moment.

Do I dare go closer to the house?

It was known that Ben had stayed the night. The thought of him and Abbi spending any time together was enough to make them want to gouge Ben's eyes out. To stay the night was more than could be tolerated. They wanted to maim him... The dogs barking from within, told them they needed to get out of there, and fast.

Uh, uh, uh... Patience is a virtue, all good things come to those who wait. They felt like telling that voice to shut the hell up, but knew it was right.

Ben and Abbi need to be separated like the need for my next breath.

How? I know! I'll need a diversion, one that removes Ben soon, for good.... they thought as they scurried away.

Dear Readers,

As a child, I would write plays that I would subject my family to. I would act them out behind my father's lazy boy using my stuffed animals as the characters. My family would sit and watch while I "performed". They had no clue what was going on, and likely I didn't either. But nonetheless they sat patiently watching. Or at least I think they did (I had no clue; I was behind the chair).

Since I picked up my first historical romance, I knew I wanted to write a book one day. The only thing that stopped me was someone saying I couldn't. That was it. I figured they were right... I couldn't write. That was 28 years ago now, and every day I regretted at least not trying. I would attempt it, but their words always reared their ugly head again, and I would give up. Finally, I decided I had nothing to lose but my regret. And so, Abbi and Ben's story came to life. I didn't need an outline, or a plot or even a list of characters. They have been with me for 28 years. As silly as it sounds, they told me their story, and it HAD to be written. And so, I invite you to come along on this journey with me. My only hope is that you enjoy reading it as much as I have writing it.

If you have gotten this far, I thank you and hope you have enjoyed the beginning of Abbi and Ben's adventures. I invite you to a preview of their second tale, Moonlit Stalker: Book 2 of Pearl Lake, The Moonlit Trilogy. ~ Tina Marie

For inquires please email at: pearllakethemoonlittrilogy@gmail.com

Moonlit Stalker:
Chapter 1

Abbi sat straight up in bed; something had awakened her. She felt a cool breeze on her chest, glancing down she noticed her lack of clothing. She jerked the blankets up to her shoulders. *Good Lord, I've never slept naked in my life…*

For a second she was confused until she felt the bed moving. Then it hit her like a ton of bricks. Memories of Ben and her came flooding back. She had been so, for a lack of a better word, wanton. She hadn't known she could even be that word, but she had. And it had felt awesome. Abbi giggled as she nestled into the blankets. She turned her head, watching him while he slept. *He's a gorgeous human being. Kind, sweet, attentive and sexy as hell. And he wants me…*

Sighing softly, she leaned over and kissed him on the cheek.

The dogs started freaking out, not their usual way of communicating, but full-blown someone is about to break into your house freaking out. She turned to her bedside table and opened the drawer, removing the laptop within. Turning it on, she sat waiting for it to boot up.

"Hey luv," Ben murmured, rubbing her back.

Abbi turned looking over her shoulder at him. "Hey handsome," she smiled. "Did you sleep well?"

Ben moved closer to her smiling. "I did, as a matter of fact," he murmured, softly brushing a kiss along her ribcage.

The laptop came alive with a beep, announcing it was ready. She typed in a password. The screen filled with a live feed from the cameras, inside and out of the house.

"That's impressive," Ben said, leaning on his arm behind her, looking at the screen.

"Ah... yeah," she said distractedly, concentrating on all the different views. "The dogs are going berserk," she explained, frowning.

Ben sat up; eyes fixed on the screen. Frowning, he pointed to the view of her driveway where a car was parked.

"Who is that?" he asked, tapping it.

"Hmm... I don't know," she said, turning her head to get a better view.

He looked closer. His brows pulled together in concentration. "Someone is walking around the car."

Abbi clicked on the screen to enlarge it. She didn't recognize the it. She zoomed in to get a better look at the person... persons she corrected herself. There were now two of them. Just then another car pulled into her driveway.

Both leaned forward, staring at the screen. The people from the second car got out and headed towards the first couple. They both had a moment of horrified realization. She tossed the laptop on the bed. Turning towards each other, Ben grabbed Abbi by her shoulders as she grabbed his arms.

"Bloody HELL! My *parents* are here."

"Oh, my GOD! My *kids* are here!!!"

They jumped up scrambling for their clothes.

Abbi glanced at him as she pulled on her sweats. "You *cannot* put your pajama pants back on!!!" she hissed.

With one leg in, Ben paused a moment in thought. "Yeah... you're right!!" He turned, running out of the room.

Abbi shoved her arms into her tank top, tugging it over her head. Pulling her sweater on, she noticed her pants were on backward.

"*Aargh*," she groaned. Whipping them down she spun them the right way.

She had no idea where Ben had gone off to. Hiding if he was smart.

She took a glance in the mirror only to see her tousled mop of hair. The memory of Ben's hands in it made her blush terribly. Grabbing a ball cap, she gathered it into a ponytail, stuffing it through the hole in the back. Darting her gaze to the monitor she saw Ava walking up the sidewalk to the porch.

"Ben!!! Where are you?" she called walking into the hall.

"Right here, Luv." He appeared behind her, zipping up his jeans.

He reached out to catch her hand. "Hey," he said pulling her around to face him. "Before we need to deal with this, know that every second that they are here, I'm thinking of you and what we shared."

He cupped her neck, his thumb trailed along her jawline as he closed the gap between them, brushing his lips softly against hers.

She kissed him back, desperate to remember the taste of him. The feel of his mouth against her own. It would be hard not to touch him for a week.

The ringing of her doorbell broke them apart. The dogs beat a trail once again to the door, in a frenzy of barks.

Ben gave her one last longing look before she turned away as she took his hand leading them into the kitchen.

"Ready?" she asked. Taking a deep breath, she walked to the door.

"Yeah," he gave a quick nod. Smiling he added, "As I'll ever be."

ACKNOWLEDGEMENTS

I have so many people that I want to thank who have come along on this journey of writing with me, so please bear with me. First, to my husband Pat, I'm sorry for drowning out your talking with music playing in my ears, but I can't listen to you and write at the same time, haha. Thank you for knowing how important this book was to me. To my kids, Jonathan and Amanda, even though you're both adults and have families of your own, you two are still my world and I thank you both for being who you are.

To my sisters, Laura and Deb. Laura thank you for not only editing my book but also for putting up with my endless rewrites… constantly. Deb, you read faster than I can write! Thanks for always believing in me and knowing from the time I was a teenager that I had this book in me, I just needed the time to convince myself!

I hope I don't forget anyone, please forgive me if I do. To my readers from the get-go who read each chapter as I wrote them. Lana Polkinghorne, Melaina Craievich, Sandra Lee, Rebecca Lewis, Mandy Wilson, Carolyn (I promised not to use your last name), and Bre Davidson, all of your kind and encouraging words truly makes my heart happy. To my fellow writers Elizabeth Stevens, Missy Elizabeth June, and Julie Baker all your feedback was awesome thank you for that. And finally, a very special thank you to two people. Jeff Mariotte, your expertise, wisdom, advice, and your patience, was and always will be greatly appreciated. And Samantha Jo Norris, if it wasn't for you lady, self-publishing was not gonna happen, thanks again for your mad formatting skills, you're a life saver ❤

Made in the USA
Monee, IL
18 December 2019

19086566R00092